# Yours Painfully

# OrangeBooks Publication

1st Floor, Rajhans Arcade, Mall Road, Kohka, Bhilai, Chhattisgarh 490020

Website: **www.orangebooks.in**

---



**First Edition, 2025**

**ISBN:** XXXXXXXXXX

**Price:** Rs.00.00



Printed in India

Swati Mukilan's

# Yours PAINFULLY

**OrangeBooks Publication**

www.orangebooks.in

# CONTENTS

# ACKNOWLEDGEMENT

First and foremost, I want to thank myself for showing up every day and staying committed to this story, carrying the significance of every word with the serious intention of bringing its message to the world. This book would not exist without the persistence, passion, and faith I held within me.

I am deeply grateful to Mukilan Sitharthan, my husband, whose admiration for my writing has been a constant encouragement. His unwavering support and patience throughout the drafting process gave me the space and strength to bring this story to life as early as possible.

I want to thank my parents for putting me in an engineering college. Although I didn't enjoy it, the experiences I gained there gave me far more strength than the imprints left by the circuit designs, eventually becoming the prime reason this story was born.

I would like to thank my parents-in-law for their unconditional support, especially in the last couple of years, which included the drafting period and the rock bottom of my life.

I'm extremely grateful to Mrs. Swati Kumari, whose words during a casual conversation sparked the very idea of this book. I'll always owe her quiet encouragement and unwavering support.

Thanks to my friends Dr. Suruthy Shanmugan and Dr. Komagal Boopathi, who stayed with me even when I chose myself. Their presence during the drafting period brought me a kind of peace that lived beyond the pages of this manuscript.

And finally, my little one who spent most of her time on my lap, sometimes as an innocent companion and sometimes as a tiny dictator, but thankfully without causing too much chaos most of the time.

# PREFACE

Stories.

I have always wondered how stories hold significance in every stage of our lives. As children, we have always been curious with our widened eyes, crafting tales out of shadows and stars. As a restless and dreaming teen, weaving stories from heartaches to hopes, now as a burdened yet resilient adult, we still narrate the battles we fought and the breakthroughs we made. And as we grow older, we become the stories we once told, along with the wisdom gained through experiences. As long as there is human existence, stories will float through life.

Our favourite melody, our favourite food, our favourite place and almost all of the ones that trigger any kind of emotions, be it sorrow or bliss, jealousy or anger, guilt or fulfilment, every feeling has a story behind it. And I always believed that the stories are what keep the world moving, like gravity, an unseen force that finds generations. They heal, they inspire, and they remind us that we are not alone. In this abundant cosmic tapestry, where every soul is a drop of dye that alters the hue of the planet with love, loss, longing and still existing, I'm adding another story, the one that has lived within me, breathed through me, and now finds its way to you in the form of this book.

I hope you sink into its depths, by feeling every line, dwell in it and let it stir the forgotten and unspoken within you. And, when you finally turn the last page and step back into your world, I hope you return not just as a reader, but as someone who carries a deeper understanding of love, pain and life itself.

Enjoy your escape—my best wishes.


Love,


Swati Mukilan.

# PROLOGUE

As the car cruised along the highway, she lowered the window, letting the warm breeze rush against her face. The sudden gust that murmured uninvited tousled her hair, making the strands dance around her cheeks. Tucking the strands back to her ear, she closed her eyes for a moment and inhaled deeply, allowing the fresh and unfiltered air to fill her lungs and laced with the earthy scent of sun-warmed roads and distant fields. Peering out, she watched the world slip by, frame by frame like an unwritten chapter unfolding before her. The towering trees on the roadside bent ever so slightly as the wind whispered through the branches. The fields stretched far and wide with golden patches and green in others, blending into the horizon where the sky met the earth in a seamless embrace.

She spotted distant silhouettes of farmers working under the sun and the flock of birds cutting across the sky in perfect harmony. As the car paced, she saw a few roadside vendors waiting for customers. The hum of the car engine faded into the background as her thoughts drifted. This journey was not just a ride to college, but was the beginning of a journey she never truly chose, Engineering had never been her dream; it wasn't that spark which kept her awake at night or the passion that made her heart race. Yet, she was gliding down a highway that led straight into a future she hadn't scripted. What pained her wasn't just the doubt of her longing, but the silent suffocation of a dream she was unable to choose, her fire-caged passion, while she chose to begin a path not hers to pave.

Perhaps it was timing. One of those eras, where engineering wasn't just a career choice but a badge of honour. A degree that seemed to promise certainty in a world where uncertainty loomed like an unspoken fear. Pretty much, a symbol of parental pride, a trophy more than anything. As she leaned against the car window, watching the world blur past, Mr Vardhan, her dad, scoffed, shaking his head as if the very idea of choosing writing over engineering was laughable.

"You can write a book anytime, but would engineering wait?" he paused and did not receive any response from her. "Engineering is the pride, dear. Or do you think scribbling some fancy words will put food on your plate? Maybe you'll become the next Shakespeare overnight?"

He chuckled dryly as if indulging a child's impossible fantasy.

"Stories don't pay the bills, but a degree does, a job does. Engineering is what matters in the real world, not daydreaming about novels no one will read".

Mrs Vardhan, her mom, who sat beside her, nodded in agreement, adding, "Think about a tangible future, dear. No one respects a writer until they are gone long, but an Engineer? That's success right from the start".

She inhaled sharply, letting the cool breeze from the window rush over her face, the only thing she could do at the moment. As the car rolled to a smooth stop in front of the grand college

gates, she took another deep breath, feeling the shift in the air. She reached for the door handle, hesitating just for a moment before pushing it open so that the warm breeze rushed in, carrying with it the unfamiliar scents of fresh-cut grass and a world waiting to be explored.

She stepped out with her sandals touching the stone-paved driveway as she took in the vastness of the place before her. A second later, she heard the gentle click of the front door opening, her mum stepping out gracefully, adjusting the folds of the saree with her gaze sweeping over the grand architecture with a mix of pride and emotion. On the other side, her dad pushed open the driver's door, straightening his posture as he took in the sight of the institution that would become her second home for the next four years.

For a moment, all of them stood still with each of them absorbing the weight of that moment differently. While it was a milestone for their daughter, who was stepping into a new phase of her life, especially in the path they had prepared for her, it was something entirely new and unfamiliar to her. She turned her head, looking at the white domes that rose against the sky, the long corridors that stretched majestically and the grand fountain leading towards an entrance that seemed to whisper a silent invitation. The architecture was a blend of tradition and modernity, mirroring the essence of knowledge and depicting timeless yet ever-evolving. Overall, the college stood like a palace of wisdom, whispering stories of ambition and dreams. It was intimidating yet mesmerising as if she were standing at the threshold of a world far greater than the one she had known.

Her fingers curled slightly, with her nerves tingling with uncertainty. This wasn't school anymore. There were no familiar corners, no childhood friends, and no comfort of the routine she had been in. It was a new beginning in a new place where she would have to carve her own space by finding new people and hectically striving to define herself beyond the girl she had been. Her dad exhaled beside her, clapping a reassuring hand on her shoulder, "Ready?" he asked with his voice filled with warmth.

She inhaled deeply, looking back at the magnificent building in front of her, and forced a smile. As they walked, a serene waterway wound gracefully through the middle of the campus, reflecting the sky like a bridge between reality and dreams, and the two fountains stood as silent guardians, their flowing waters whispering a song of development and resiliency, while the vibrant and well-kept surrounding gardens seemed to echo the footsteps of innumerable students who had walked these paths with dreams in their hearts and minds full of possibilities. The building's size, with its ornate arches and well-balanced design, emanated an air of order and grandeur.

From a distance, the entire place appeared almost dreamlike, standing tall as a symbol of progress, yet grounded in its purpose, to nurture and illuminate every soul that walked through its doors. There was a quiet fear in her heart, but also a growing excitement. The college didn't just look like a place of learning. It looked like a place where life would unfold, where she would evolve into a version of herself she had yet to meet. And in that moment, standing in front of the towering institution, she knew that this wasn't just a building. It was the beginning of a new chapter, one she was forced to abandon her dreams.

# THE GRAND INAUGURATION

A bin was filled full of crushed paper plates and disposable cups near one of those black jumbo sound speakers that just stopped crackling at high volumes which flawlessly amplified the talks and especially those highly energetic well-rehearsed declarations like, "You are the budding engineers of the city", "You will build the tower buildings that the clouds are gonna kiss", "You are the one planting the seed to revolutionise the technology" to which the entire auditorium echoed with contagious applauses for the same statements that they probably gave last year, a year before that and maybe the year before that as well.

Some still believed those statements and took notes of them with furrowed brows and utmost determination. At the same time, it was a joke to candidates who had siblings and neighbours who had graduated as engineers from the same college in previous years and were now working in the IT industry without any discrimination between departments. But, still, they daydreamed of having most of the buildings in their city constructed by them, after all, it's nice to dream of ourselves heroically adding such cinematic effects with the favourite background score from movies, especially when someone at the front is hyping it with a microphone. It costs nothing, and why not? Undoubtedly, it is the smartest way to escape those boring inaugural speeches.

Some parents felt appreciated and satisfied for admitting their children into an engineering college, even though it was totally against their will, just like many parents who can effectively turn their children's passion into frustrations, typically in the name of 'giving them what's best for them'. Some of them cared a cypher about the speeches and were involved cleverly in hooking friends for the next 4 years. Some of them just woke from a short nap, those sleep- deprived creatures who slept amidst the chaotic buzz. While a few gave competitive glances that said, 'Yo, challenge accepted!'

Exactly as you think! That was the induction ceremony of an engineering college, which ended after a solid 3 hours of literal 'dumping' with a series of aerated dreams and no-go resolutions, at least in this eternity stacked upon like a bucket list. And finally, they arrived at the most awaited event.

The grand buffet.

The amount of tuition fees the students had paid was undoubtedly reflected in the fragrances, colours and lights of the banquet and the steam rising from platters of golden-fried samosas, rich, spiced gravies, and desserts that shone like the light at the end of the tunnel. So, the real energy kicked in, even for those who pretended their sincerity with erect postures and humble nods to all the talks professed on behalf of the management. To be forthright, the banquet is the place where the actual engineering was happening. Everyone from the teaching and non- teaching faculties to newly joined and their parents indulged in finding the most schematic route to boundless free food, making strategies to stabilise their plates with a scrupulous plan to stack as much food as they wish without toppling the carefully contrived towers of samosas, pastries and those enigmatically looking desserts.

The dignified professors who delivered well-prepared, professional monologues are now caught underhandedly for the extra servings of mushroom fries or stuffing more cheese and sauce onto their plates when they thought nobody was watching them. Pragmatically, they had to be hungry to perform those motivational speeches and the ceremony arrangements they made for the management. By engaging in assiduous debates on whether the fried rice or butter chicken masala was the true star of the spread, parents who came to provide moral support for their kids unwittingly gave up their facade.

Near the dessert corner were two students engaged in a precarious yet wild duel for the final brownie slice. One of them, who was cunning about it, won the match, while the other lost, hesitating on the social consequences of just snatching it, merely stipulating the soft skill that the engineer has to learn along with technical kinds of stuff, 'pay no heed to societal standards for peace'.

Following the seemingly never-ending motivations for revolutionising the future, everyone in attendance, from the dean to the parents, shared the same immediate goal, which was to maximise their "plate-to-stomach" efficiency. This is the kind of real-time issue that is less dealt with in engineering textbooks, irrespective of the number of editions.

Among the bustling crowd, a vaguely lost girl stood like mislaid sunshine radiating in a bright yellow kurta, adding to her lustrous soft skin that shimmered under the banquet hall's golden light, catching the air with every hesitant movement. She was a plush-like stuffed toy brought to life that anyone would want to squish and squeeze to feel it's comforting warmth. She was either too thick or too thin and 5 feet tall. Her shawl, the delicate, mischievous little fabric, didn't give up for the 17th time to slip away from her shoulders as if it had a will of its own to flee into the chaos of the buffet line like a prankish spirit, quite imbecile to lose out on such spared luck.

Saira.

A sharp nose, and above are those pair of eyes. Phew!

Bold silver cosmic balls that held an inescapable gravity beyond their deep, dark irises, whispering an entire story in a single glimpse. Yet, she was obscured with hesitations since she entered the spread. She lingered behind her parents, who stood just ahead of her, effortlessly claiming their place in the feast, while she was caught between wanting and waiting. The moment stretched like the days of hardship. There was something inexplicable pressing down on her, an unseen curtain made of self-doubt rather than magic. What if they observe me? This is the auto-pilot mode for any girl who was petted by her parents, emotionally creating the pressure to be under a 'good girl' label as per society's standards. And Saira easily passes that criterion; otherwise, why would she be landing in an engineering college now?

And perhaps, if she could break past this hesitation, she would remember that she was made of sunlight, warmth, and soft magic, and she belonged here just as much as anyone else. But yeah, it's hard for anyone to realise their self-worth fighting against their excellent people-pleasing qualities. So, for her, eating in public was an extreme sport.

A thousand unanswered questions twisted in her chest. Could I take too much? What if I make a mistake, spill something, or worse, get caught? She was vulnerable to self-doubt and judgments because of the weight of unseen eyes, whether they were real or imagined. How much is too little, and how much is too much? She cannot be too fast and appear avaricious or too slow and hold up the line.

If taken insufficiently, her mother would murmur, "That's it?"

When taken too far, "Don't we feed you at home" is sensed as a weird, inexpensive attempt to get free food. Her hesitancy was exacerbated by the clatter of plates, the murmur of conversations, and the odd forced laughing from students who pretended to be having fun. Her mum urged her. "Go, get anything", her dad added in a low voice, "And don't begin with dessert". They presumably wanted to showcase their way of petting and caressing their daughter in public.

Saira moved along. There stood a waitperson behind the counter, looking bored, and his hand sluggishly hovering over a serving spoon. She reached for a plate but then panicked. "Should I take rice first? Or the Paneer nuggets? What if I miscalculated the proportions and ended up with a weirdly unbalanced plate?" She hesitated so much that the server guy sighed dramatically and said, "It's not an engineering exam now". Great, now there was an audience for her to please. She grabbed a spoonful of something she wasn't even sure of and then found refuge near her parents, just when another student leaned toward her and whispered, "It feels like we signed up for an illusion".

For the first time that day, Saira smiled.

Most of them completed the sumptuous feast in an hour, rested with an ice cream bowl, and chilled at the cafeteria outside the banquet. Saira's dad said to her, "Saira, this is it, the one final mark. If you work hard to complete this course, you will be settled in life forever".

Sarcastically, 'the forever' she had been hearing since she entered her 10th standard, and then 12th standard and now.

Her mom continued, "Saira, I can't wait to see you graduate here with a university rank here on the same podium 4 years later".

Saira wore a reluctant smile, wondering if he would urge her to ace the bank exams after she qualified for this. After all, what else is a 'number ninja' who was born in the same city, brought up in the same city, studied in the same city, and worked in the same city, and his homemaker housewife would even suggest? That genie in the bank who granted financial 'wishes' based on credit scores never tried to understand what wishes his daughter had in her heart. Of course, it can't be laid upon him alone; she was never outspoken beyond her 'conditioning' as well.

Then, the topic shifted to commenting a little on how they organised the ceremony and more about the hostel facilities they arranged for Saira's comfortable living. The hostel was located 3 km away from the college, with a college bus stop 500m from the hostel for any buses from that college, and that was very likely why he was blowing his own trumpet.

In the midst, there came a voice of doom from that speaker in the corner, which said, "New joiners are requested to assemble in the corridor in Block 3", and that's when Saira's dad hugged her and wished her the best for her next venture. Saira's mother cautioned her for safety during her stay here and promised her that she would make a phone call to her every day before she slept. Saira and Mom hugged each other before she took leave from there.

Saira was worried and nervous, resisting the long, really long 4 years of stay away from her parents in a new city, which was 6 hours away from her native and that too for the first time. But, she was never given a choice and neither did she stand for herself anytime since childhood. At times, life gives subtle hints in such nuances, but we fail to comprehend that we are living in the same compulsive cycles. Neither did she understand that either way to pursue something she didn't like or choose to do what she liked had something in common, which was to stand for herself. The poor girl waved her hands the last time for her parents, who gave a last sight before they raised the window glass at the entrance gate.

The whole gang of students spotted here and there in the ceremony and banquet were all together in the corridor. The ones who made friends during the ceremony continued sharing their school life stories. And those who took notes were standing alone with some sincerity around them. While a few boys over there tried to initiate some chit-chat with the girls, they were impressed at first sight. After 10 minutes, a group of professors came who called out students enrolled on their departments and took them to their respective classrooms.

There were instances when the professors decided to throw the ball to the students to play and pass on among themselves, just to watch the show and pass the time. The moments when the professor decided to bunk the class hours. That afternoon was one of those instances.

An 'introduce yourself' session.

An ostensibly flawless question, yet that potentially triggered a surge of existential anxiety throughout the room. One after another, students rose to respond to the most misleading yet straightforward inquiry: "Who am I?" likely causing them to question whether they had chosen an engineering route or a spiritual journey, as both are enigmatic. Something that began as a routine 'name-hobby-why engineering' response quickly spiralled into a full-scale spiritual crisis that even most spiritual people themselves are struggling with.

Some hesitated as they pondered their existence at the moment, while others made up for it with intricate speeches that left the class uncertain if they had just experienced a TED Talk instead. One brave soul took the minimalistic attitude—"Hi, I'm Avin. I exist", probably the one who hadn't yet recovered from the induction day speech doses since the morning.

The group also included the overachievers who felt motivated during the ceremony and took the opportunity to share their life stories with the class, while many of their peers had already checked out after the extravagant, vibrant meal, accompanied by the jumbled speeches of several students present. Perhaps due to such experiences, engineering students often bring this burden into their interviews as well, suffering from the "Introduce yourself" syndrome.

It's dreamy and inspiring when students from schools have different ambitions in a class, but it's so funny when the group of engineering students still had different ambitions to become astronauts, YouTubers, musicians and whatnot. It wouldn't be surprising if, in the future, engineering became the primary qualification for individuals seeking to enter any profession, which might be justifiable since those who endure the rigours of engineering can handle anything life throws at them. However, these anecdotes are far more entertaining than those who admitted they pursued engineering simply because their parents insisted, which created a melancholic melody amidst the humour of these adults.

"Fantastic introductions, everyone!" the professor concluded.

This was just a brief glimpse into how to get through engineering while also having a bit of fun, a rare day from the usual days filled with classes and lab work. Sports day serves as the second exception, while annual college day is the third.

Starting from the following day, the daily grind of 'engineering' began to assert itself. Within the maze of academia, college courses often resemble a series of monumental challenges meticulously crafted to challenge the endurance of even the most patient students, likely based on the philosophy of assessing individuals who may need to engage in lengthy research and experimentation, in case they contribute to actual projects post-graduation. Those endless lectures, do we ever exhaust our array of metaphors?

A soothing song reveals all the turmoil, usually at the heart of the energy, yet feels oddly still, reminiscent of a cemetery. The melodies gradually evolve into an abstract piece of art featuring incomplete spirals and partially composed phrases, and the pen nearly halts at the ultimate surrender. The struggle to stay awake is 'real', and some brave backbenchers had fully embraced defeat with their heads down on their desks, lost to another realm.

In this revered place, most modern doodlers begin their journey to discovering their new love for life. How cherished! Some stay in the class physically only to not refrain from getting their attendance marks. While extra-

extroverts act like sleeper cells who get enthusiastic only during group activities or group projects. They desperately need people to perform. And then some girls and guys who can skillfully hide the big piece of candy in their mouth while still nodding their heads, even for the phone call the professors answer during the class. Then some take notes of everything, including the 'achoo' of the lecturer who struggles with a cough and cold, while some never maintain any notes; they were probably the last-moment champs who thrive on the photocopies of textbooks from the library.

And just when they think they've made it through the day, the lecturer surprises them with a 'rapid quiz' that causes panic to spread like wildfire. For some, it is to face the frailty of their lives and reflect on their decisions that they may have the opportunity to become philosophers. For some, it is a 'betrayal moment' whose books turned easily into pillows. Leaving some with frantic looks and some with silent prayers, crouching under the desk slightly to avoid attention.

Saira is slightly different; she finds herself trudging to the classes every day like a lone figure leaving the hostel room with the sluggish determination of someone who questions their life choices with every step, even after it's too late to get into such analysis paralysis, silently roasting the uncle who unsolicitedly recommended engineering to her dad. But, besides her liking, Saira has the innate nature of giving her best in what she is doing. Her notes were the bible for professors that would pass on to generations like a 'legacy' with succinct explanations and thoughtfully selected colour codes, which are symphonies of organisation.

She tackles quizzes and exams with a calculated approach, treating each assessment like a battle she has already conquered, and she faces them without fear. She shines like an academic amid a multitude of individuals merely getting by in this epic tale of engineering existence, where procrastination reigns supreme, assignments trigger deep reflections on existence, and lectures become trials of stamina.

As a mystery wrapped in bound hardcovers and highlighters, she captivates her classmates with both intrigue and admiration. They would forever regard her as the legendary figure who triumphed over academic challenges through sheer determination, clever tactics, and unwavering belief, even if they never fully grasp the depths of her dedication.

This was the undeniable pattern in the life of an engineering student that played on repeat like a favourite song until the ultimate challenge, 'the semester exams', had arrived, as though the everyday struggles of engineering life weren't enough of the world.

# THE MONSTER WAS COMING

With some last-minute changes and a lot of fervent prayers, they hoped to somehow tame the monster they had been unwittingly preparing for. But before even facing the question paper, there was the first challenge, 'The Hall Ticket Hunt', a ritual every student had to go through navigating endless queues, filling out unnecessary forms, pleading with office staff who wielded hall tickets like sacred scrolls upon the tuition fees due, or misplaced ID cards at the worst possible moment, some panicking when they saw their name spelt wrong because apparently like their entire existence depended on it. Others only discovered today that they had not paid the exam fee, which prompted them to make an urgent side trip to the administrative building. There was actual tension.

Once the hall tickets were finally secured, next came the 'Hall Allocation' panic. The seating arrangement list was posted like a government result, forcing students to push, squint, and decipher their fate. "Dude, what's 'Block 9, Room 202h, does this place even exist?" which probably would have been the classroom next to the one we belonged to, like anything in life where we never cared to know until it was needed. A typical 'human-engineer' behaviour. Some found their names listed next to their best friends and considered it a small victory, while the unluckiest ones were sent to a parallel universe, far away from all familiar faces.

And then, the final dread—the 'Forgetting' everything that was perfectly memorised just an hour ago made an instant undo. It was the hot seat moment, mind wavering between getting 'decent scores' to 'just passing is enough'. If there was one thing engineering students knew well, it wasn't about acing the test, but about surviving it. There were combinations in this cloakroom, too. Some flip through the pages that they never turned in their lifetime, some pleading with their friend to narrate it for them, and some ask for extra pens or scientific calculators. A few warriors have already conquered it with attendance and internal marks that they are so precise that they can attend one-fourth of it to qualify for this if they choose their battles.

As the final bell rang, the students lined up according to their registration number and went inside their respective halls. The invigilators checked for the ID cards and hall tickets and let students in one by one. And then the exam started. In one such quiet room was Saira, who sat on the last row with her forehead tightened in focus and her pen racing across her paper in a rhythm with the ticking away time.

"2 hours more", said the invigilator.

As she filled the final line of her answer sheet, she raised her hand, signalling the invigilator for an additional sheet. The invigilator, the brisk young man with a stack of sheets in one hand and a blue ballpoint pen in the other hand noticed it.

Saira, unsure of the notice of the invigilator, felt anxious as the moments stretched, and just as she was about to raise her hand again, she looked up and their eyes met. The invigilator, who walked methodically between the rows intending to reduce the wait time, walked straight through the column with continued eye contact. Something felt time freezing to Saira, and for moments, the rain-like sound of the flipping papers and the sound of pens dropped and picked constantly by one or the other student on the writing table, everything faded away, except the boot stamps of the invigilator and the heartbeat of Saira. He came closer and handed over the sheet carefully. As he heard, 'sir', he directed himself towards the other side.

Saira, conscious of her role, averted herself and continued focusing on the exam. A long pause.

"Half an hour more", he said.

When he had some minutes free, he picked back the attendance sheet and counted it against Saira's writing desk to find her name.

He saw "Saira Vardhan".

Time was up, and he had started collecting it quietly, checking the right number of sequences, when he came near to Saira's desk, he received her script gently and asked,

"Saira Vardhan?"

"Yes, sir", she nervously said.

He looked at the paper again and went to the next desk.

Bundling the papers together, he turned to leave, casting one final glance at her. She came out of the silent graveyard to find the college that had moved in its customary chaos, the college buses were honking, students rushing, and the sun indolently dipping behind the skyline.

The invigilator boarded the bus after verification, sealing, reporting and handing over the scripts to the exam office, mind preoccupied with nothing in particular, when his eyes instinctively landed on a familiar face. There was Saira, sitting by the window in another bus 10 feet away from his, indulging in a deep discussion with her friend after every slow sip of water from her bottle. It probably should be about that cursed 16-mark question those professors loved twisting into a nightmare because she spoke with the same intensity she had while writing her exam- her expressions shifting between frustration and determination.

He hadn't expected this, hadn't even thought about having the possibility of seeing her again and was enthralled to see her again framed perfectly in the dull glow of the bus window, oblivious to the silent gaze watching her. Or so he thought, because it's not even a challenge, a woman always knows. The moment his glance lingered a second too long, Saira's instincts kicked in. Mid-conversation, she turned slightly with her eyes scanning the space beyond her window and landed straight on him. He caught her eye back, but continued gazing at her from there. Saira wondered about what this look could mean, but it was quickening her heartbeat, something which she had never felt before. It had a sense of profoundness, and she did not want to get rid of this spark that was ignited in her. She gazed back.

Maybe because it was the last time they had got this chance to see each other? He thought. Usually, the invigilators are allocated consciously from other colleges.

"Or maybe the next semester? If luck favours", he said to himself.

Their eyes locked in a silent, captivating gaze until they took separate paths outside the campus. It was the same day and night. The sound of the overhead fan hardly registered in Saira's consciousness as she lay on her bed in her hostel room, gazing up at the ceiling. She was stuck in those two minutes, the hallowed glances that had somehow untangled something inside of her while the world around her changed. She had previously made quick eye contact with strangers, glanced briefly at classmates, and even had silent understandings with instructors, but this was different. She was uneasy about this in an inexplicable sense.

This had lingered that she had the sheer curiosity to know more about this eccentric invigilator, at least for now, his name, which college he taught at, subliminally calculating the probability of meeting him again. But another part sighed at the mere thought, her engineering life was already exhausting, packed with lectures, assignments, and the impending weight of semester exams, while he added an unsolvable mystery to the equation felt both thrilling and overwhelmingly tedious.

She exhaled, shutting her eyes as though that would help her shut out the pull of that moment. Nevertheless, it stayed, replaying behind her eyelids like a scene etched into time as vivid as ever. If only she had caught his full name, if only she had glanced at the ID card hanging from his neck, maybe caught a glimpse of the college logo, then she could have done what any curious, overthinking, slightly like a smitten engineering student would do —dive into Facebook, Instagram, or even LinkedIn, scrolling endlessly in search of a familiar face. All she had was that stupor, that maddening, wordless exchange that refused to fade. Nothing else except that memory of how it had felt. She flipped like a pancake and rolled over her bed with her textbooks lying open but unread beside her. Engineering had taught her to solve equations, analyse circuits, and optimise algorithms, but nowhere in her syllabus was there a formula for deciphering an eye contact that had shaken her to the core.

# WHEN THE VEIL FALLS

A year passed, tangled in exams, assignments and those hostel foods that existed purely out of obligations with a faint taste of regret. They dealt with $n$ number of classes, $n/2$ number of laboratory sessions, three guest lectures, and one symposium and then the final monster one more time. Saira was expecting the invigilator but was fooled by the management's staff allocation.

One fateful sunny afternoon, Saira and her friend, Anya, walked toward their block, nonchalantly discussing the regimen of college gossip, upcoming tests, and the never-ending struggle of surviving engineering. But just as she turned the corner, her steps faltered. Through the open door of a classroom on the ground floor, she saw him.

The same invigilator.

The young man with whom she shared profound eye contact, accidentally once and intentionally once. The one who made her night sleepless, flipping over the bed and squishing the pillow with so many popping questions inside. He stood at the fore, dictating notes to a batch of students, flipping through a book that had seen better days. Its pages hung loose, barely clinging to the spine like autumn leaves stubbornly refusing to fall. He read from it with the kind of focus that only came from familiarity; he probably didn't even need the book, he just kept it out of habit.

Saira couldn't believe it for a while. It was the unexpectedness of the moment or the out-and- out absurdity of seeing him again in her college. Her stomach did an involuntary flip. A year had passed, yet that strange pull remained as if time had folded in on itself to bring her back to that first glance. Saira froze mid-step. Her brain short-circuited for a moment. Was this real? Had she finally lost it, seeing him everywhere, conjuring him out of thin air? Because this was not supposed to happen.

Her mind muddled up and fished around for logic. Semester exams never had the same college staff as invigilators, even if they had, now is not a time for that, yet here he was, in her college, standing in a classroom full of students, dictating notes as if he belonged there. However, of any kind, it truly sent a shiver down her spine. It wasn't just the sight of him, but the fact that he was already watching her with a steady and unbroken ray of gaze without hesitation, without any flicker of surprise, just that similar quiet intensity that had stolen two minutes of her life in that exam hall.

And in that moment, an unnerved thought crept into her mind. Did he chase me back here? It was groundless, out of the question. But something inside her whispered otherwise. Because just as she had never quite shaken off that first encounter, something told her, neither had he.

But, this time, without realising it, without intending to, Saira let a small smile escape, just the faintest curve of her lips, but enough. Enough for him to notice. And he did. His gaze flickered, not in surprise but in recognition, like he had been waiting for this moment, like it was the missing piece in whatever strange equation had been forming between them.

For a brief second, they afresh existed in an autonomous reality, one where stolen glances had answers, where time hadn't played its savage game of keeping them apart for a year. Yet, the weight of reality bore down once again, the mismatched pieces of their story that refused to align.

She was a student.

He was a professor.

She belonged to this college. He did not.

They were happy within, but confusion still hung between them like an unsolved riddle. What was this?

A coincidence? A twist of fate?

Or was it something they weren't ready to name just yet?

With all the questions swirling in her mind, Saira did what she had to; she kept walking, following her friend into the classroom. Her body moved on, but her mind refused to.

The loop of why, how, and what does this mean?

Played on repeat, tangled with the way he had looked at her, the way she had smiled without realising it. Three long, post-lunch lectures stretched ahead of her like an eternity. The kind where time slowed, the professor's voice became background noise, adding to the ceiling fan that seemed to move at half speed.

She knew.

It wasn't just the usual classroom drowsiness.

She was waiting. Waiting for the final minute, the last class to wind up, the moment when she would step outside and board her bus because something in her told her she would see him again. For reasons she didn't want to name, but she wanted to.

Saira secured her spot by the window, her eyes subtly scanning the sea of students boarding the buses. But this time, he was nowhere to be seen. Her fingers drummed restlessly against her bag. She tried hard to tell herself it didn't matter, but the slight weight in her chest said otherwise. She found herself looking again through the windows, across the campus, weaving through the crowd with an invisible lens search. Still, nowhere.

The bus engine roared to life, a signal that they were about to leave. And just when she thought the moment had slipped away, she saw him. Right through a narrow space like the hair's breadth near the entrance, the ex-invigilator stood at the bike stand, heroically struggling with his helmet strap.

The most mundane thing, yet somehow, at that moment, it felt so cinematic. And then it thumped her; he had seen everything. He had seen her quest for him, the slight disappointment on her face when she didn't find him and now, he was watching the way her expression shifted from shock to something unexplainable as their eyes locked once again. He hadn't missed a second. His gaze had followed her the entire time, tranquil but knowing. Saira's breath caught. Something stirred inside her; it wasn't just those trite butterflies, but an entire storm moving from her stomach to her chest to every nerve in her body. Something was happening.

Outlandish.

Undeniable.

As the bus rolled forward, Saira clenched her fingers around the edge of her seat, forcing herself not to look back. She thought if she did, it would feel like utter surrender, handing over a piece of her heart to a man she barely knew, a professor, no less. An absurd thought, but she was caught in this invisible pull, resisting the urge to turn, to steal one last glance for that day. The same girl who once hung back to take food at a buffet, afraid of being judged, was now on the verge of breaking every carefully built rule in her head over a man whose name she hadn't even spoken aloud. It was besmirched with her. Stoning her from within.

A war between logic and something much, much deeper. He, who was locked in this battle against an inanimate object, had his jaw tightened with a bead of sweat rolling down his temple. He swung his leg over the bike and revved the engine; the sound echoed through the parking lot. Was the moment his? Was this a minor detail in his otherwise legendary exit of a confident man who had just conquered Mount Everest? Well, conquering a woman's heart is no less.

Saira, indeed, has gone topsy-turvy. Yet somewhere deep inside, she was undeniably happy. She was falling head-over-heels for a professor whose name she didn't even know.

But did it even matter? The thought of seeing him every day, sharing the same air, existing in the same proximity as the magician who had cast a spell with just a gaze, was enough to ignite something within her. Since having left home for college, her hostel room had always felt like a prison, a place where loneliness echoed louder than anything else, and only to fight it, she had buried herself in engineering, drowning in textbooks, assessments, and deadlines, convincing herself that this was what she was here for. Weekends were her escape.

Home, family and warmth. But just to return every Monday to the same cold and monotonous cycle. But that day was different. That night, the silence of her room didn't suffocate her; she welcomed it. Embraced it, because it allowed her to relive, rewind, and cherish those divine encounters, the stolen glances, the unsaid words, and the undeniable pull.

Phew! And for the first time, she didn't mind staying back in this so-called prison. Because now, she had something worth waiting for. He made her feel different. Every morning, Saira found herself waking up with an excitement she couldn't explain, not for lectures, not for assignments, but for something else. For him. She wasn't sure if it was happiness, curiosity, or something else entirely, but it made her pick out her outfit with more thought, tie her hair a little neater, and leave her hostel room with an avidity she had never felt before.

Engineering still sucked the soul out of her. Assignments still drained her, but staying in her hostel room, trapped in its silence, felt worse because out there, somewhere on campus, he existed, and that was enough to make her count the hours, watch the crowd, and let the day pass just so she could maybe, just maybe catch another glimpse of the professor who had unknowingly turned her world upside down.

A romance took root in her heart, with his gaze cascading through her. She relived it a million times before this happened, and love wove deeper into her being.

Saira had had enough of the unknown.

She wanted to know his name, his department or anything that could make him feel less like an illusion and more like a person who existed beyond fleeting glances. But she was in a bind. If she asked anyone, it would raise questions. The questions she wasn't ready to answer. So, she did what any smart, determined girl would do. She went to the library. The college recently released its annual calendar during Sports Day last week, listing all the faculty members across departments. It was her best shot.

Flipping through the crisp pages, she found last year's list and compared it to the recent one. Her fingers glided over the names in rhythm, her pulse quickening as she spotted differences; three new names had appeared this year.

Bravo, the target is approaching!

One of them had to be him. She stood frozen, staring at the names. Double-guessing which one belonged to the man who had unknowingly rewritten her entire world, she made sure to memorise all three, just in case. Splendid, mission almost done. She shut the calendar and placed it back neatly, exhaling in confidential victory. But as she turned, her breath caught in her throat.

He was standing right behind her. A soft gasp slipped past her lips.

The one who had always existed in stolen glances from a distance was now right here, so close that she could almost hear his breath. The library air felt heavier, charged with something unspoken. Her heart pounded, an unfamiliar rush spreading through her veins. Was it excitement, fear, or something beyond words? She was stunned.

For a moment, she forgot the mission, the calendar, and the names she had just memorised. All that remained was the undeniable presence of the man who had unknowingly taken over her thoughts. And over the next few nanoseconds, reality snapped her back. What if someone saw them? What if someone noticed the way she was frozen, caught in his gravitational pull? And then, as if the universe had decided to grant her wish without her asking, she spoke. Stood erect with an effortless, masculine grace, his voice cut through the silence.

"Vedha". A pause.

"Vedha Sagar".

Yes, that was one among those three names she encircled and memorised a minute ago. The name she had been hunting for was now right in front of her, gifted to her directly from the man himself. And at that moment, she realised she was never really in control of this game.

She had no clue what had just happened.

She knew the name now, but the way it was handed to her so effortlessly, so directly, made her question everything.

"Was it just a casual introduction?" "Or did he know?"

"Did he sense that I had been searching for him, flipping through pages, hunting for a name that belonged to him?"

"Or worse, had he been following me all along?" She thought.

And that thought sent a shiver down her spine, but not in fear. It was something else. Something thrilling.

"Was he on the same page as me?"

"Had he already figured out the chaos he had stirred within me?"

All these questions fueled her nervousness. His name still echoed in her mind, and before she could react, before she could even decide what to feel, Vedha had already turned and walked away, like how he mysteriously appeared, leaving her there, who was caught between excitement and thrill.

Slowly, she left the library, her feet moving on autopilot while her mind spun in relentless loops. She walked towards her block, completely trapped in analysis paralysis, a tug-of-war between logic and emotions, between what she wanted to believe and what reality could be.

"Did he figure out that I was searching for his name? "

"If he did, was this his way of letting me know that he knows?" "And if he had a problem with it, wouldn't he have confronted me?"

"Warned me for stalking a professor? But instead, he had just said his name." Nothing more. No accusations and no judgments.

Just a gift, his identity, handed over like he was fully aware that she was looking for it. Or was there something else in his mind? Saira couldn't shake the feeling that this wasn't a coincidence.

No, Vedha wasn't just an observer in this story. He was playing the game, too. In her haze of confusion, she somehow reached her class, barely registering the words of the lecture. She just needed the day to end, to escape into the quiet of her thoughts. Between the 20-minute bus rides from college to the hostel, she must have whispered "Vedha…" a pause "Vedha Sagar…" at least a million times in her head.

Each time, the name felt different. Sometimes heavy, sometimes light. Sometimes a mystery, sometimes an answer. By the time she reached her room, she was carrying a blush she couldn't wipe off. She freshened up, let out a deep breath, and stood in front of the mirror. Looking at her reflection, she imitated his voice, his stance, the way he had said it so firmly.

"Vedha."

Then, tilting her head slightly, she repeated, "Vedha Sagar."

She was losing it, along with those chuckles that her lips let out. Hysterically. Completely.

She can't stop herself from being excited that she has the biggest clue now, like almost knowing where the key to the treasure is. The name. That was enough for anyone pursuing engineering, after all. No matter how many Vedhas existed in the world, she had the confidence of a detective on a mission, and with the same confidence, and she contemplated more based on what had happened to her that day and slept off like a new 'dad'. The sleep that was absent for a year since her first-semester exam.

The next morning, she came to the class cheerfully like the one who won the tournament. She was glowing, and her day-scholar friend, Anya, who sat near her since the beginning of college, found her unusually happy for the day and asked her, "Uh-hum, what's so special today?"

She couldn't control the smile that came along with the soft crimson blooming on her cheeks. Anya felt strange but had some clues. "Come on, there is something", she insisted.

Saira and Anya shared a kind of bond where they never tried to outscore each other, possibly a rare scenario that existed between two studious and highly capable students who would ace anything without breaking a sweat. All they had done was the sharing of snacks and rants and have the occasional existential crisis during the semester exams.

"It was an Invigilator." Saira mused.

"An invigilator? So, a professor?" Anya adjusted her glasses, already intrigued. "Yes, ask me no more", Saira blushed.

"Can't help it, is he from our college?" Anya continued.

"Yeah, must be recent", Saira said, looking out somewhere, making it casual to others.

"Oh great! What's his name? Which department? Is he also on the same page?" Anya added.

"His name is Vedha, I saw him in one of the classes on the ground floor, the rest you have to help me with, Anya", Saira grinned ear to ear.

The professor came in; there was a serious two-hour class before that 15-minute break. "You like him?" Anya asked, handing Saira a piece of chocolate she had broken off. "I don't know for sure, but this is shaking me in, said Saira.

"Ok, it's stupid to talk more on this with just this information", said Anya.

"No, Anya...." continued Saira, before Anya said, "Come, we will go to that ground floor class", tossing the piece of chocolate from the tongue to the roof of the mouth.

The 'girl' friends who help with such a 'crush crisis' are so underrated and not spoken of equally to boys. But, they are the authentic souls, the personal search engine assistants who guide us on "how to intentionally run into our crush without looking like a psycho", enduring all the late-night monologues about the way everything happened, nodding like a therapist who secretly deserves a raise.

Saira felt supported and went along with Anya.

As they reached the class, Anya looked for familiar faces, and there she spotted her busmate calling her girl. Anya asked, "Hey, hi, which classes are handled by which staff?"

It was not a question to be so sceptical about because it was a routine, a curious ask by every senior who had passed that previous semester. So the junior busmate continued,

"Engineering maths by Shakuntala ma'am".

"Oh, she! She never leaves a stone unturned", giggled Anya. "Absolutely", wondered that busmate with a feeling of relief.

"Go ahead", said Anya, giving a glance at Saira.

"C++ by Dr. Mukesh Imran and Vedha sir for…." the busmate dragged, adding some tension for Saira.

"Got it. Vedha sir for engineering Graphics", said the busmate and continued, "And the engineering physics by…"

"Stop, who's that Vedha, sir, newbie?" asked Anya, like she had never heard that name.

"Yeah, senior, but he is such an easy-going, chill professor, making technical kinds of stuff so fun and unworried, I like him so much"

Anya threw a teasing smile at Saira, who was keen on every word that the busmate threw off.

"Ok, ok, it's time for our class, I will continue talking more on the bus", said Anya, and they both rushed to the class with the needed information, smartly making it casual.

They made it to the class with a sense of victory, "Everybody likes him, it seems", and Anya teased Saira.

Saira flushed.

"Tomorrow, I will come with the notes of his class hours", assured Anya. Saira nodded like she had no words to thank her.

And then came the evening ritual. Saira curiously waited at the window corner to catch Vedha.

Eye contacts are usually unsung, high-vibrational music. But it's electric. That unspoken dare, stolen glances, and the almost look-aways are more intimate than the touch itself. A kind of tension in its purest form that leaves the heartbeat stuttering, something so raw and real that it can barely be explained in words to anyone unless they fall in love.

Vedha, who walked from the admin block with his helmet and backpack, saw Saira sitting near the window, yet crossed her bus to arrive at the bike stand like he didn't see her. Saira loved this game.

The next day, Anya came with the notes, which had the timings of that particular class hour Vedha was handling and pulled Saira's leg with her mockery skills before she gave it to Saira.

"So, how long is this secret mission gonna be? Are you waiting for any divine intervention, or do you have any plan?" asked Anya.

Saira shot her a glare and said, "Ok, it's not a slow burn". "Oh really", smirked Anya.

"At this rate, you're probably gonna make your grand confession only at his retirement party", continued Anya.

"Shut up", blushed Saira.

"Everybody likes him is what the report says, it's up to you to decide and act, that's all I can say", said Anya.

"Anybody can like him, but who he likes is what matters", smirked Saira.

"Oh, so you don't need my 'The Vedha Plan' I tailored for you", Anya groaned dramatically, throwing her hands up.

"What? Do you think I can get down on one knee with a ring at this campus?" asked Saira.

"Well, not exactly, but you still have to confess, I don't know. If you don't speed things up, I just might do it for you", winked Anya.

"Yep, you have a point", said Saira. "I always do", Anya winked again.

# FALLING OUT OF FOREVER

Anya made Saira think ahead. After her evening ritual, when she reached her room, Saira refreshed, pulled away her phone, and opened Facebook.

Because, using or not, who doesn't have a Facebook account? It's practically a savings bank account; everyone has one, just in case! She typed in Vedha Sagar and scrolled through the endless list of names, filtering through the ones that didn't match her image of him. And then bingo. There he was.

His profile displayed an old picture, probably taken during his college days. He looked a little younger. She stared at the screen, inclining her head as though attempting to journey through the pixels and connect this iteration of Vedha to the one who had softly spoken his name to her in the library. A smirk twined on her lips, "Found you, magician", she whispered to herself.

There appeared his bio. She tapped on it to add something beyond just his name. 28 years old, his college name, and the institution he worked before, which shows he hadn't updated his career shift recently, he did. Each detail felt like a little piece of the puzzle falling into its place. She then started to scroll through his feed, which showed some dog pictures that looked like the puppy he was probably nurturing at his home. Then she scrolled down a little more to find that one group picture, one of his friends, had tagged him in it. It shot up her curiosity, and she clicked into it. There was a group of friends laughing and standing together, but her eyes didn't take in all of that, but the married couple in the centre, among both, had that one familiar face, standing with ease.

Vedha.

Her breath paused, and she felt something twisted in her stomach. Why did this picture feel like a warning sign?

Her hand shook as she tried to instinctively zoom, praying or pleading for the mistake of blur or a trick of the pixels.

Not.

It was Vedha. Vedha Sagar. The heaviness of this realisation hit her, collapsed her, and shattered her all at once. Her ears were lugged with indescribable pressure, and her stomach clenched.

She kept saying, "No, it has to be something else", in her mind. "This doesn't mean what I think it does".

But her mind played cruel, gathering the pieces together of the puzzle, but her heart refused to.

"Why does this hurt this much?" Tears trembled down her cheeks. She tried to blink away, yet she could find the picture static through her blurry haze. Nothing could console her.

She clutched her phone tighter, hoping something would change. But the reality is unmoving, just like him in the picture.

The clock showed 10, then 12, and then 1. She couldn't reach her day scholar friend at those strange hours as well. The solidity in her cheek remained unmoved like the storm refusing to pass. It was too much for a 20-year-old girl to go through.

She cried all night, thinking about how cruelly life had played a trick to make something bloom in her, only to rip it from its roots. She could barely control the thoughts that circled back to those moments in the library, to the way he had stood so close, to the way his name had rolled off his tongue with no hesitation.

Vedha Sagar.

The name that had felt like a doorway into something magical now felt like the final nail in the coffin of her foolish hopes.

"Did he know already?"

"Did he sense that I was searching for him?"

Did he deliberately hand me the only key I needed to uncover the truth like a quiet warning wrapped in a single word, 'Vedha Sagar'?"

Or still worse? Was this his way of telling me that I was building castles on sand?"

She kept asking all these while her mind became a courtroom where every memory, every glance, every fleeting moment was called in as evidence.

"The first undeniable moment in the exam hall was the silent language their eyes were locked in. Then, the evening bus, when I caught his gaze ten feet away. A year later, through the open doorway way when his dictation faltered just enough for me to notice that he was looking at me, not noticing the hanging pages of his torn notebook. That evening at the bus corner, when he watched my search for him, he saw the disappointment in my eyes before I found him, standing right there as if he had been waiting all along. Were these just coincidences?"

"Was I a fool to believe in the magic I had felt?" she moaned.

Saira's heart rebelled against the truth her eyes had seen. That picture, the smiling couple and the group of friends, the reality that shattered everything, making her ponder how it could erase what she had felt in those moments. She couldn't deny the photo. But she also couldn't deny what had been shared between them, the spark that had rewritten the rhythm of her heart. It was too much to untangle for the girl, wavering between two truths that refused to make space for each other.

The dawn arrived like an uninvited guest slipping through the curtains, contrasting with the storm inside her. Saira lay still, staring at the ceiling, feeling as if the weight of the night had pressed her into the mattress. Her body refused to move; her mind refused to rest. The silence of her room, which once felt like solitude, now felt like suffocation. Staying here meant drowning deeper into the ache.

Saira forced herself up, but the day-to-day routine of getting ready for college felt mechanical, detached 'brush-shower-dress-pack'. Everything happened on a single switch as if her body knew it had to keep moving even if her heart didn't want to.

College wouldn't heal her, but at least it would give her something else to focus on. The lectures, the assignments, the meaningless chatter of her classmates, maybe they would serve as background noise to the grief still circling inside her. Maybe, if she kept moving, if she let the day unfold like any other, she could breathe through the weight pressing against her chest. So, she left, not because she wanted to, but because staying would hurt even more.

That morning, Vedha was standing in the bike stand as Saira's bus rolled in the entrance gate, his eyes instinctively searching for her. And there she was leaning against the window, her face a quiet storm of exhaustion. Red, weary eyes. A pink-tinted nose. The unmistakable remnants of a night spent drowning in emotions too heavy to contain.

He exhaled sharply, "So, she knows?" thought Vedha. Then the classes started.

"I had figured it out without him having to say a word, without putting him in a hesitant position, without demanding explanations? But then, why had he done this? Why allow something to begin if it was never meant to go anywhere? If he was already bound to someone else, why did he let the spark between them grow into an unspoken fire?" A million questions popped into her head, making her lose.

"Saira", the professor called her. No response.

"Saira" Nothing.

"Saira, are you okay?"

As Anya tapped on her arm, Saira blinked, snapping back to reality, finally registering the professor standing in front of her. But there was no effort to mask her pain, no attempt to wipe away the sadness spilling from her eyes. She was wrecked, and for the first time, she didn't bother hiding it.

"Take a break, Saira". "Anya, make sure she's okay", said the kind professor. "Yes, sir", said Anya, already reaching for her wrist.

Nodded to the professor and returned to the lecture.


Anya wasted no time, dragging Saira out. "Alright, Saira, let's process what happened, tell me?" asked Saira.

Saira finally let all her weight out. Anya, who listened with arms crossed, slowly embraced her. She realised it was no small pain; it was driven to the stage that Anya, with her quick wit and sarcastic armour, didn't know how to fix it. For a moment, Anya deeply wanted to punch Vedha for not just hurting her best friend but for letting that silence stretch for so long that Saira had to sit alone with her feelings until they became a wound she couldn't hide in front of everyone.

She had never seen Saira breaking down before everyone, as pointed out by the professor, that day. But, at the moment, she could pull Saira towards her and give her a tight hug, she realised.

"Hey", Anya whispered.

"You are not alone in this, okay? We'll figure it out. I wouldn't let you walk through it alone, I promise", said Anya.

Saira managed the next hour class before lunch.

Then came an hour's break for lunch. Anya and Saira decided to sit alone in a corner of the cafeteria to have some private space from their already curious classmates.

Anya said, "Saira, for a second, even I thought, what if this is not true?" when Saira showed the group picture to her.

"Tell me, what do I need to do? Can I go ask him directly?" Anya continued. "Ask what?" Saira said, wiping her tears.

"That, why he would stalk and indulge in this after his marriage, at least a professor is not supposed to do this, no?"

"Everything is already dead, and it went far beyond what we can do about it", Saira added.

And when they were talking, Vedha was coming out with his lunch box and noticed Saira with her friend, sitting in the corner. He noticed her friend's eye burned with a silent fury while Saira had tears held up in her eyes.

And then, after three hours of class, came the evening. The evening had no sense of interest or excitement. Yet, Vedha stood at the bike stand, looking for any glance that Saira would throw at him. But she didn't.

Saira reached her room almost with no motive to exist, lay on her bed and wept for hours. "Tak- tak-tak", there was a knock. Saira wiped her tears to see if it was the laundry lady or the neighbouring junior who usually comes for doubt clarification. To her surprise, it was Anya, with a big tiffin carrier in her hand.

"Is this your room?" asked Anya, stepping into the room.

"What about the warden? How did you come in?" asked Saira. "My dad spoke to her", said Anya.

"I know you wouldn't have eaten yet. So, I brought food from home, my mom's special parata, come", continued Anya.

"Anya…" dragged Saira.

"I didn't eat yet, either", said Anya. "Go refresh and come. We are talking it out, wiping it out tonight", added Anya.

Saira gave a small, forced smile with tears in her eyes.

They both ate, and Saira said, "Anya, I hadn't even begun dreaming of a future with him, hadn't allowed myself to build castles in the air, yet here I am, wrecked. As if the universe had handed me a beautiful gift only to snatch it away before I could even touch it".

Anya spoke firmly, "Saira, I'm not telling for your sake or you being my friend, but I feel deep in my heart that he must be so unlucky to have lost you" She continued, "That guy and his integrity are neither suiting him in his profession nor you"

Saira broke," No, it's not even him. I have always lost what I desire more in life, Anya, it's been a common thing that I haven't yet been prepared for"

Anya felt a lump in her throat; now Vedha hadn't just broken her. She realised it was something deeper, something that broke Saira about love itself, and Anya couldn't digest this fact. She paused before she could continue.

"Ok, listen, Saira", started Anya.

"This pain, this heaviness is not just yours, he has a share, too. Let's give him back his. You needn't carry it for him", she said.

"I don't get it", Saira swallowed.

"See, he played it. He also contributed to it; otherwise, why would he have to come and tell his name in the library that day? So, let's go ask him, why would he say his name to a stranger student, knowing very well what situation he is in?" Anya stopped.

"Anya, how can we ask him something out of context, what if it points out to me for my assumption?" Saira defended.

"So, you think you assumed this?" asked Anya. "Noo…." cried Saira.

Anya held her hands and said gently, "Saira, I can't see you like this, you somehow were pulled into this; the game is his or fate's, but we have to wind this up to move on", she continued, "I know it's hard, I can feel you, but holding it forever without any comprehension must be heavy for years, please do give a thought, I will surely be with you", said Anya.

"But he is married, and it's way too late to talk to him now", Saira cried heavily.

"He must have been married when he stared from the open doorway, too; he must have been married when he said his name in the library, too", added Anya.

Both were exhausted by the weight of the conversation and eventually let the silence lull them into sleep. Saira curled up on one side of the bed, and Anya lay beside her with one arm lazily draped over the pillow to keep watching over her friend.

The next day, they both started together from the hostel. Vedha, as usual, in the bike stand, saw Saira on the bus with her friend, who threw a cold stare yesterday. But he was bothered about Saira and looked at her. Saira did not even turn to his side.

Their internal exams were around the corner, but studying felt impossible. Words blurred on the pages; equations seemed like meaningless scribbles, and every attempt to focus dissolved into a haze of confusion, while her mind raced back to every moment, every stolen glance, and every silent exchange that had felt like a language only they understood.

She had always been a disciplined student, someone who feared even the slightest scolding from a professor. But now, she barely cared. The girl who once sat in the front row, who submitted assignments before deadlines, who spent sleepless nights preparing for tests, was now staring blankly at her notes, unable to recall a single concept.

One of her classmates nudged her. "Saira, are you okay? You've been holding the same page for ten minutes."

She blinked, realising she hadn't turned a page in her book. "Yeah… just tired," she lied, forcing a weak smile.

Anya observed this and asked, "Saira, this is eating you, are you realising it?" "I know. I tried to pull myself back, but I failed", said Saira.

"Would he admit it? Would he deny it? Would he pretend nothing had ever happened? Continued Saira.

"We cannot assume it by ourselves anymore, Saira", said Anya. Anya continued studying.

"I wasn't asking for explanations. I didn't want to know why life had played such a cruel trick on me. I only want one thing, 'truth'. Was it real? Did he feel it, too? If the answer was yes, I could live with it. I could blame fate, curse destiny, and cry until the pain dulls. But if it was all in my head, if I had built castles in the air from nothing but a passing gaze, I needed to know that too", Saira thought.

After all, he was not just another twisted 16-mark question she could move on from with a little bit of weeping and late-night cramming. So, for the first time in her life, Saira decided to rip off the bandage by herself. Saira knew she couldn't afford to fail, but she also knew she couldn't live with this lingering question. So, she made up her mind. She decided to ask him. Her heartbeat drummed against her ribs.

"If I didn't do this now, I would never be able to study, never be able to focus, never be able to move forward", Saira said to Anya.

"Should I accompany you?" asked Anya. "Doesn't matter", said Saira firmly. "Great, go now", said Anya.

# A RECKONING WITH REALITY

With determined steps, she made her way to the staff room, only to find it empty. There is no sign of Vedha. A small frown creased her forehead, but she didn't falter. She turned back, climbing down the stairs and scanning the corridors until she spotted another professor. One was busy organising a sports activity for a group of junior students. Taking a breath, she walked up to him and, with as much composure as she could muster, asked him, "Sir, how can I meet Vedha sir?"

The professor barely glanced at her before replying, "He's in 2nd-year mech."

She was about to say thank you and leave when he stopped her with a look, his curiosity piqued. "What for?" he asked.

A tiny storm of panic swirled inside her, but she didn't let it show. Instead, with the smoothness of an expert she never knew she had within her, she lied effortlessly.

"Vedha sir told me to get some model papers from him."

It was a brilliant performance. A Casual, confident, and, most importantly, 'believable', that even she was impressed by her delivery. The professor nodded, accepting the explanation without a second thought. She thanked him and walked away, feeling the heat of her pulse but not allowing it to show on her face.

She had no idea where exactly the '2nd-year mech' was, but she knew it had to be in that building. So, she walked past the ground floor, scanning door after door, climbing to the first floor and then the second. And that's when she saw him.

Through the open doorway, Vedha stood at the front of a classroom, lecturing. His presence commanded the space effortlessly, his voice steady, his gestures precise. She didn't pause to think, didn't worry about the dozen curious eyes that turned toward her the moment she stepped in front of the entrance.

She stood there, unmoved, unbothered, her gaze fixed on him. Not like a student seeking a professor. Not like someone who had wandered into the wrong class. But like a woman standing at the edge of something bigger, something undefined, yet something undeniable. A silent question in her stance, a quiet defiance in her posture.

She was not a student looking for answers. But a woman seeking justice.

Vedha froze mid-sentence, the chalk in his hand hovering inches away from the board. His eyes locked onto Saira standing at the entrance, and for a fraction of a second, the entire class ceased to exist.

Then, without hesitation, he turned back to his students, muttered something about continuing the notes, and strode out with an urgency that made it look like he was responding to an actual emergency.

The moment he stepped into the corridor, "Saira," he said, softer this time.

His voice was low but firm, filled with the kind of concern that didn't belong to a professor speaking to a random student. It was as if they had known each other forever, as if their connection existed before this moment, woven into the spaces between unsaid words. Saira was caught off guard. She had expected formality, hesitation, and maybe even mild annoyance at being interrupted. But instead, Vedha stood before her, steady, focused, not attempting to pretend this was a first-time interaction. As if he had always known she would come to him one day.

She took a shaky breath. This was it. If she didn't say it now, she never would. "Did you also feel it?" she finally asked.

Vedha's expression didn't change, but something flickered in his eyes. A recognition. A knowing.

"Feel what?" he asked.

His voice carried a hint of confusion, but his eyes— deep, searching eyes—were already betraying him. They held the truth he wasn't ready to say out loud.

"Don't...." she whispered again, her voice trembling.

"Don't act like you don't know what I'm talking about", she paused.

Vedha exhaled, looking away for a brief moment before returning his gaze to her.

"Saira..." he said again, but this time, his voice carried something heavier, something closer to regret than denial.

The weight of everything unspoken hung between them, thick and suffocating. He didn't deny it. He didn't confirm it. He just stood there, caught between the truth and the consequences of admitting it.

Saira swallowed hard and spoke again, her voice trembling. "Was I mad? Had I imagined it all?" asked Saira.

Tears welled up, spilling over before she could stop them. Without thinking, she shifted closer, slipping behind Vedha, shielding herself from the dozen curious eyes peering through the window, as if hiding could make the moment any less real and continued, "I needed to know now, not why, not how, just if. If you had also felt the same, I could at least blame fate instead of myself. I want to be a fool with certainty, not a fool drowning in hope, I could mourn what was never meant for me and move on", she pleaded.

At that moment, Vedha's eyes shimmered with trembling tears, but he somehow managed to hold them back. He glanced down, rubbing the back of his neck, a sign of hesitation she had never seen in him before. It was as if, for the first time, he was unsure of himself, of his words, of what he was supposed to do.

He exhaled slowly, then looked up at her with a forced steadiness and said, "Sorry, I don't understand what you are talking about during my class hours".

The words came out measured, distant, and almost mechanical. But Saira wasn't fooled. The weight in his eyes, the unshed tears he masked with indifference, the way his voice wavered for just a second before turning cold—none of it matched what he had just said.

She stood there, frozen, as if those words had knocked the breath out of her. Not because she believed them but because she knew the truth was buried somewhere beneath them.

She understood that it was a waste of time to defend him for something he was determined to deny, especially in front of a bunch of juniors. A flicker of anger sparked within her, not just at him but at herself for expecting anything different. Straightening her posture, she swallowed the lump in her throat and forced a small, indifferent smile.

"Okay, thank you for responding, Vedha sir," she said, her voice formal, deliberately stripping away the warmth and closeness she had just spoken with moments ago.

And with that, she turned around and walked away, leaving behind the weight of unspoken truths and a man who had just denied the very thing that had set both their souls on fire. She walked towards her block, her steps heavy yet determined. The corridors felt longer than usual, the air thick with an ache she couldn't shake off.

By the time she reached her classroom, the lecture had already begun—fifteen minutes ago. She hesitated at the door for a second. She was never late for class, never the one to walk in after the professor had started. But today, everything felt different.

Taking a deep breath, she pushed open the door and stepped inside. The professor barely glanced at her as she walked to her seat, but her classmates exchanged curious glances. She ignored them all, sliding into her chair, staring at the board, yet unable to focus on a single word being said. Her mind wasn't in the classroom. It was still standing in front of Vedha, replaying his words, his hesitation, and the unspoken truth that lingered in his eyes.

Anya lifted her brows and signalled, "What happened?" Saira exhaled. Anya exhaled back.

Vedha, who had just confronted a brave woman with a heart too pure to hide her truth, found himself struggling to focus. The weight of Saira's words, the fire in her eyes, and the quiet pain in her voice lingered in his mind, refusing to let go.

Yet, he pushed his limits, determined to maintain composure. He turned back to the class, continuing to deliver the lecture as if nothing had happened. His voice remained steady, his expressions unreadable, but his mind was elsewhere.

Every word he spoke felt mechanical, every sentence forced. He glanced at the notes in his hand, but they blurred before him. He stole a quick breath, tightening his grip on the chalk, grounding himself in the routine of teaching. But beneath the surface, a storm raged within him. The image of Saira walking away, her voice turning formal, her warmth replaced with distance, unsettled him in ways he wasn't prepared to admit.

That night, both were drowning in the weight of their unspoken truths.

Vedha, though he had gone to bed early, found no sleep. He lay there, staring at the ceiling, replaying every second of their encounter. Saira's voice, firm yet trembling, echoed in his mind. The way she called him 'Vedha sir', a deliberate shift, a wall built in a single moment, stung more than he had expected. He clenched his jaw, shutting his eyes tight, but it was of no use. The guilt, the longing, and the helplessness refused to leave him.

Saira, on the other hand, felt something close to relief. She hadn't gotten the words she wanted from Vedha, but she had returned the weight he had placed on her heart. She had faced him, asked him what she needed to, and walked away without begging for an answer he refused to give. It wasn't closure, but it was something. A small, bitter victory in a war she never wanted to fight because she dared and made a move.

Though the pain lingered, the heaviness inside her felt slightly lighter.

Saira forced herself to focus on exam preparations, pushing through the weight in her heart. She sat with her books, her mind wandering now and then, but she pulled it back each time. Somehow, she made it through the exams. When regular classes resumed, she tried to settle into the routine, avoiding the memories that once consumed her. She convinced herself that reliving something that would never be hers was only going to break her more. So, she chose distraction—studies, assignments, anything that kept her from slipping back into the emotions she had barely survived. However, Anya made it a little easier for her with her comic skills.

Whenever she found Saira dull, she joked about it as 'gravity gone wrong'; these two nerds who make fun of technical stuff were the weird pieces in the classroom.

All seemed to settle down until there came an evening that brought the chaos back.

Saira's fingers trembled as she held the phone. She blinked twice, making sure she wasn't imagining things. But no, it was real.

*"I wish it all happened, but I was so unfortunate"*

The number was unknown, yet she knew it must be Vedha to have sent such words. She tapped on the message with a pounded heart, where the inbox displayed the unknown number, with a display picture of Vedha.

The words stared back at her, carrying a weight she wasn't ready to bear. He didn't say much, but it was enough. Enough to confirm what she had always felt between them. Enough to make her question if life was playing a cruel joke.

She read it again. And again. And again.

Vedha, the man who had captured her heart with a mere glance and remained silent when she confronted him, was now admitting, in the most restrained way, that something did exist and that he felt it, too.

But the word 'unfortunate' made her stomach churn that he was bound, tied to a life she wasn't part of. Her fingers hovered over the keyboard, uncertain.

"What was I supposed to say? Ask him why."

"Tell him how wrecked she felt. Demand answers he couldn't give? Or just let it be?"

She asked herself, and eventually, the pain she had tried so hard to suppress surfaced all over again. She did not know what to do at that moment; she called Anya.

"Anya…" said in a crying tone.

"What happened, Saira, are you fine?" earnestly asked Anya.

"Anya, Vedha has left a message for me on WhatsApp, and I didn't know what to do with that", said Saira.

Anya couldn't control the anger that bubbled up in her mind at Vedha.

"Whatever message it is, it's no longer needed for you, Saira, block that guy right away", ordered Anya.

Saira cried silently without a word.

Anya sensed Saira and controlled her impulse, and got back to him, saying, "Saira, listen to me, you went and confronted him on something he also contributed to. He had enough audacity to make you feel everything and yet refused to take accountability for it, such a red-flagged head he is. Now, he is sending a text after you seemed to never care about him, and his intentions are so bad with this timing".

"It sounds exactly as you say", cried Saira.

"Then why would you cry for that guy, now?" asked Anya.

"Anya, it's not about his intentions to me now. It's about the reply he had given to me. I asked that I never wanted to know why or how, but only that it was mutual, so I could blame fate and live the rest of my life. And he had given me what I wanted, and now I can't stop crying thinking about this cruellest play of fate", cried Saira.

"Baby..." dragged Anya.

"I know, this shouldn't have happened to you, Saira. But now, it's entirely about how we play with it. It cannot cost you your peace. Cry as much as you want, I will be with you, but leave that guy on blue tick, let him know that you moved on", Anya added.

"Sounds fair, I will do that, Anya", promised Saira.

"Do not keep thinking over it, call me back when needed. We will talk tomorrow in college", said Anya before she cut the call.

While Vedha had a sleepless night with the blue tick, he received it like Saira, who had been trapped in her looping thoughts. As much as she wanted to erase him from her mind, her fingers betrayed her. She opened her contacts, hesitating for a brief moment.

"What should I save his number as?" thought Saira.

A thousand names crossed her mind, the names that reflected her pain, anger, and longing. But none of them fit. Because, in reality, he was nothing more than what he had always been: a professor, a passing figure in her life, a man she was never meant to have.

"Vedha Sir. "

Nothing more. Nothing less. That was all he was. That was all he would ever be. And so, with a deep breath, she saved his number and put the phone away.

A couple of days passed, and Vedha found himself waiting for a message, for a glance, for anything from her. He stood at the bike stand as usual, hoping she would look back at him just once. But Saira never did, not even accidentally. Yet, she was painfully aware of his presence. She could feel his eyes on her, the weight of his silent yearning pressing against her back. She was trapped in a cruel tug-of-war, neither to question a married man about his feelings nor to suppress the ache in her heart. She had no right to be upset about his marriage; it had happened with his consent. And yet, it felt like fate had been unkind, placing her in a story where she had no choice but to lose.

Vedha had managed to keep himself composed, at least on the surface, until that moment in the 2nd-year mechanical class. Saira's question, the way she had framed it, and the weight behind her words had shattered him into pieces inside. She hadn't just asked; she had demanded an unspoken truth, a truth he was too bound by circumstances to admit.

*"I needed to know now, not why, not how, just if. If you had also felt the same, I could at least blame fate instead of myself."*

Those words echoed in Vedha's mind relentlessly, like a haunting melody he couldn't turn off. Every time he tried to focus, her voice replayed in his head, drawing him back to that moment, to the weight of her pain, to the unbearable finality in her words. It was cruel, yet true. She was asking for closure, something he had selfishly withheld. He felt like he had left her drowning in unanswered hope while he stood on the shore, watching. As he realised how much he had left her in the spiral of uncertainty, in silent suffering, how much he had been too cowardly to either hold or let go, it killed him the most.

As days passed by, her silence was louder than any confrontation he could have imagined. It was a mirror, forcing him to see himself the way she might see him now.

A week later, after their practical exams, Saira and Anya were spotted sitting on a stone bench in the middle of the ground, watching the football game unfold in front of them. Anya was giving her running commentary on the match that was happening, and Saira was laughing at her usual comics until he stood there behind, calling, "Saira".

Saira and Anya turned back to him. Saira stepped back in pain while Anya crossed her arms and stared at him.

Vedha's eyes were so tired and weary, indicating no proper sleep, at least for quite a few days. Still, Anya showed no pity.

"Saira, I want to talk to you", Vedha said in a feeble voice. "Saira, it's time, we can leave from here", said Anya sternly. "Saira pl…" started Vedha.

"Saira", interrupted Anya with stressed intonation.

Saira picked up her bag and moved near Anya while Anya took her backpack to leave from there. Vedha clearly understood how protective her friend was of Saira, and although he felt happy about it, he still wanted to talk to Saira. But they left. He waited on the stone bench, thinking Saira to reach him back, but she didn't. He waited at the bike stand in the evening, and still she didn't. He was broken and upset, blaming his fate for putting him in such circumstances. Yet, he didn't give up that evening; he called Saira over the phone, twenty times at least.

Saira saw how the call rang and cut off every time with tears in her eyes and pain in her heart. She conveyed the same to Anya the next day, putting Anya into a little thought on why he had to struggle this much to talk now, especially knowing it was already dead, to sprinkle water on the dried plant. She also noticed how it affected Saira, who hadn't been talking like usual. She remained silent in her world since Vedha approached them to talk for a while. All these were running through Anya's mind, yet she was sceptical if Vedha would complicate it even more, making it much more complicated for Saira to recover from because she had already seen her struggling to get rid of the memories.

Another couple of days passed before Vedha met Anya on the ground, who stayed late to practice badminton after class hours.

"I don't know what your name is...." Vedha dragged. "Anya", told Anya.

"Thanks. Anya, if you were this protective of Saira for her wellness, I'm sure you would have known everything that Saira has in mind", said Vedha.

"You have no reason to know what Saira feels for you, you should disappear like a tragic hero, SIR", stressed Anya.

It was an expected prick to Vedha, but still, he continued," I promise I won't be back or disturb her after that", he assured Anya.

"Oh, just another one of your excuses to pull her back in?" Anya let out a bitter laugh.

The second prick burst from his eyes a little. Anya observed it, and it didn't feel like an act to her. "Maybe the finality in his voice", she thought.

She felt she could have some compassion for him. "Tomorrow, the same time, the same place", whispered Anya. "Thanks, Anya", said Vedha.

"But just 10 minutes, nothing more", Anya continued. Vedha nodded and walked his way to the bike stand.

The same day, night, Anya called Saira, who was eating her dinner.

"Saira, I met Vedha in the evening", said Anya with a careful, measured voice, like handling something fragile.

"Oh", Saira replied uninterestingly. Saira, anyway, knew it was too late and was way too tired of thinking about it.

"What, you show any excitement?" queried Anya.

"I don't know what else to say to this Anya", said Saira.

"I know, right? But he wants to talk to you for 10 minutes" Anya waited. Saira remained silent.

"Vedha seems poor like you, Saira, almost lost something that he can't name. I'm neither sure where this is leading us nor why this happens, I'm leaving it to your choice now", Anya said firmly and added a good night.

Saira went sleepless, effortlessly once again. Vedha neither slept, either; he was intrigued whether Saira would choose to meet him tomorrow or not.

The veil of night was lifted by the first rays of sunlight. Saira knew this meet-up wouldn't change anything in her life; there was no magic after it ended, and no words could rewrite their fate now. She was smart enough to comprehend it would only linger as a bittersweet ache, a reminder of something that could never be a part of her life. Yet, she firmly believed that Vedha acts upon the burden she had passed to him, that he wanted some relief from it, like she once had felt, before confronting him. She was worried about the suffering it would have kindled in Vedha's heart and wanted to just support him while he tried to recover from it.

So, she decided to meet him. This time, not for her, but for him. A quiet closure, a silent farewell. She chose her outfit carefully but without extravagance. A simple colour, one that wouldn't demand attention. Neither too bright nor too light, elegant enough to blend in, just enough to feel like herself and retain the dress with loads of memories every time she would choose to wear it, because that's how much Vedha meant to her, despite how less of a person with integrity he was.

Unsure of her decision, Anya waited for the evening. "You are coming with me", said Saira to Anya.

Anya sighed.

"I have nothing to talk about in person, Anya", Saira added. "Are you sure?" asked Anya.

"Yes", nodded Saira. An unusual firmness in her decision.

Within minutes, Anya was at her side, her presence was a quiet anchor. She didn't lecture, didn't question. She just walked beside Saira, like she always did, like she always would. They both reached the ground at the same spot at the same time.

Vedha, who had been stuck in the last hour of class, rushed from the staff room with his bag and helmet. He reached the same spot with steps heavy with regrets and the weight of all the words he should have said before it was too late. He saw Saira standing there, her expression neutral and unreadable, beside her, Anya. He kept his backpack and helmet on the mud and approached Saira. As he walked nearer, Anya said to Saira, "I will stand a few feet away," and walked ten steps forward. Saira sighed at her. Anya stood at a place with folded hands and turned back to Saira, giving a confirming sigh.

The evening sun hung low, casting elongated shadows across the ground. In the distance, the faint sounds of practising football echoed across the field. In a world apart, with the whispering breeze charged with the heaviness of unsaid words and unresolved pain through the dancing trees, stood Vedha Sagar and Saira Vardhan, a couple of feet apart, facing each other. The initial silence was broken when Vedha spoke, "Saira", in his feeble voice.

Saira stayed quiet.

Vedha cleared his throat, emitting a throaty sound, and continued, "It was not just you, I felt it too. In my heart, in my nerves, in fact, in ways I cannot even jumble the words and make a meaningful sentence out of it".

Saira refrained. He had not said something she didn't know before.

"I felt it all. I felt everything exactly as the fleeting moments are romanticised in the books and films. I felt time slow and trapped in it. It was huge and different to me, who had never experienced anything much emotional in life. I was curious about who you are and wanted to know your name, and that was exactly why I confirmed it with you as well, if you remember. And then I thought, "This is it, I'm never gonna see you again", but I saw you the same evening on the bus. It said 'She is the one' from inside".

Saira's eyes shimmered. Vedha continued.

"The mistake was only mine; the mistake wasn't in feeling it. It was for not opening up to you when I should have. The fault was mine..." with tears trembling..." the fault was mine for letting you slip through my hands when I realised what you meant to me", said Vedha.

"You should have", thought Saira and moaned, but remained silent outside.

"But then, it was a fateful game or what? I had no choice, Saira. I wasn't given the space to think, to feel. One moment, I was figuring out my life and the next moment, it was decided for me", he added.

Vedha's voice was steady, but deep inside it lay the tremors of something profound that had been locked away for too long.

"I had to shift my home after my marriage", he began again.

"And so I joined this college for my convenience, but then, the fleeting moment I had with you once, struck me hard on the very first day. Coincidentally, that same day, I saw you through the open doorway. At that instant, I doubted myself; I doubted if you had also felt the same. I was like you, too. I wanted to know if it was all in my head or if fate was playing a cruel trick", with a shivered voice, "And then in the evening..." his voice dropped lower and heavier, "In the evening, when you searched for me, and when I saw the excitement in your eyes the moment you found me, I crumbled. I broke into pieces that can never be put back".

He swallowed, "I couldn't contain the shatter, couldn't consume this lost opportunity, and kicked the bike so hard that the engine roared to life like a scream I couldn't let out"

Saira held her shawl tightly with tears uncontrollably rolling down. He continued.

"And the day when you came and confronted me, your pure heart and each word you spoke that day tickled all the vibrations that rattled in me, giving me tremors. Only I knew that each twist of my wrist was my desperate attempt to drown out the ache that refused to be silenced", he cried.

He exhaled sharply, "Nothing could silence it until now".

"I was a coward to have not confessed to you my heart then. And still, a coward to neither hold on nor to let go", he wiped his tears.

Saira had mistaken the roaring engine as an unspoken celebration, a silent confession wrapped in the language of revving pistons, but the truth hit her like a cold metal against the bare skin. It was his way of breaking, way of drowning out the ache, of silencing what he couldn't say aloud. This realisation hit her heavily, and she sat on the stone bench with her head down, sobbing uncontrollably.

"Saira", he continued with his eyes filled with redness and regret

"Saira, I had enough punishment for not confessing my heart to you", he said with a voice barely above a whisper, "that's why I lost you".

"This feeling of losing something precious and pure is gonna suck me for my entire life", he swallowed. "But, I'm not another man who can't control his temptations, I'm not a married professor pursuing a girl much younger than me. You don't need to excuse me. You don't need to forgive me for my cowardness, but it's my desperate plea for understanding", he cried heavily.

He continued, "The thought of you seeing me as a man with no integrity, like someone who toyed with your emotions, is unbearable to me" he bent to his knees and howled.

Saira couldn't control herself anymore, and she bawled with her palms closed on her mouth. Anya, with her tightly folded hands facing the opposite, had been crying her eyes out too.

Three of them were engulfed in a torrent of tears.

Vedha stood up, pulling his kerchief from his pant pocket, and continued, "Saira, you were not just any girl, you are someone with a heart so pure, a love so intense that even fate itself had hesitated before shattering your illusions. I already lost you, but I couldn't bear to leave behind a version of myself in your mind that wasn't real. Let it be with truth," his voice lowered, "not with the belief that I was a man unworthy of your love", he broke down in tears.

He wiped his tears with his kerchief.

He looked at Saira. "Thank you for giving me a chance, Saira", he said and walked away from Saira.

Saira sat with a river of tears.

He faced Anya and noticed her reddened eyes, too. Anya let her folded hands go loose.

"Thank you, Anya, I wouldn't forget this help", said Vedha, taking his helmet and backpack and walking away.

The air was filled with salt and lightness. Something that lifted the burden, and it felt lighter than before, with a little more confirmation of the so-called "fate-play".

Anya, who listened to all the words with her crossed arms, took a slow breath before turning to Saira.

"He just blew away all the red flags I had stuck on his head with just fifteen minutes, Saira", said Anya in awe.

"Aren't guys who cry before a girl just not the green flag but the green emblem of divine masculinity itself?" She tried cracking a joke that eventually added more tears to Saira. Sometimes jokes fail even in well-versed situations, comedians place the right jokes in the wrong place.

"I'm sorry, Saira, I can't figure out who missed whom now", said Anya with utmost compassion.

"I hate this life play", murmured Anya in a serious tone.

Saira sat still and cried continuously until she felt like returning to her room. And the heaviness in the breeze vanished slowly.

From that night onwards, Saira felt the newness in the air, something unfamiliar yet strangely comforting. It was not joy, it was not sorrow; this time it was clarity. The clarity is in a way that neither changes the past nor anticipates the future based on the present. The clarity was not about rekindling what was lost, it was about understanding why it could never be, allowing Saira to step forward without the weight of unanswered questions dragging her behind.

A serene acceptance that life had already made its choice for her, the choice that Vedha was not for her, at least in this eternity. The weight of all unspoken words, the endless 'what-ifs', the silent longings were all gone, not because she had stopped feeling for him, but because she had finally got some answers from him, to comprehend enough to build that acceptance of reality, the kind of acceptance of fate, that doesn't erase their feelings but reshapes them.

Vedha, on the other hand, also felt a strange sense of relief, as if he had finally unburdened a weight he had carried for too long. He cleared the misassumptions that lingered like a shadow over his character. He felt the aftermath settling in his bones because he finally spoke his truth, not withholding anything in the name of duty, obligation, guilt or regret.

And now, in Saira's mind, he was not the one who played with feelings or let love slip away without a fight, making Saira understand that he had felt it too, just as profoundly as her, but unfortunately, helpless that life had moved faster than his heart could catch up.

Neither of them could forget each other, they can't. That's how some people etch themselves into our souls in ways we cannot erase them. And some love stories are written not in the stars, but in the spaces between them, simply beautiful, fleeting but never meant to be held forever.

But what would Saira do? Will she choose to step away, not as an act of abandonment, but as an acknowledgement of this fated game? Will Vedha choose silence, not out of coldness, but out of respect for the life he was bound to?

Might their paths ever cross again?

# A LOVE ON THE BRINK?

It was the next morning. Saira woke up with a lightness she was unaccustomed to. The past still existed, but it no longer held her hostage. She took a warm shower, letting the water cascade over her like a cleansing ritual that purified not just her body, but at the soul level too.

She closed her eyes and took a deep breath as drips moved across her skin. That day, it felt different, free and much lighter. She freed herself from the burden of unresolved questions and quiet anguish for the first time in what seemed like an eternity, not just washing away yesterday's fatigue, but also sweeping away the heaviness she had unwittingly retained. Even though she did not recognise the melody, she hummed gently because it felt right. Once she felt rejuvenated, she wrapped herself in her towel and stood before her wardrobe, taking an extra moment to choose her outfit, not to impress, not to hide, simply because she wanted to.

A soft, flowing fabric that felt like her freedom. Her fingers moved through her hair, styling it with intention, not compulsion. Then she stepped out of her room and the hostel. Everything about her, her steps, her choices, and even the way she breathed spoke a quiet yet powerful transformation with a deeper realisation that some stories don't need an ending. They need only acceptance.

As Saira's bus drifted into the campus like a wave washing ashore, she found herself gently gliding along with it. The familiar college gates loomed ahead, the same ground and the same crowd, but did not bother to see the bike stand aside. She was excited about her classes, her usual routine, her practical exams and the semester exams. She was simply present. Neither was Vedha at the bike stand, waiting for her bus to roll in. There was no stolen glance, no quiet anticipation hanging loose in the air. The morning unfolded as any other, unremarkable, indifferent, moving forward as if nothing had ever happened. Just a new day, wanting to be lived.

She attended the class lively, her laughter at Anya's jokes felt more effortless, and her focus was sharper. And then, without realising it, five working days had passed. Five mornings of walking up without the ache in her chest, five evenings of walking past familiar places without expecting to see him and five days of proving to herself that she could move on from something that once felt unbearable.

The universe has a peculiar way of circling back to unfinished lessons by testing us on the things that we thought we had moved on from, poking, prodding, and whispering through coincidences, until we don't just claim to have moved on, but actually do. Yet, most of us aren't usually mindful of circumstances that pull us back into such traps, and without mindfulness, we fall for it. It was one such evening when that test arrived, unannounced.

"Sure, Vedha sir. We will join the meeting", said a professor over the phone, walking to the pedestal.

A name dropped too effortlessly, and a memory nudged awake like the universe was watching her reaction, waiting to see if she would flinch, if she would break, or if she would truly let go. And there she got stuck, poor young girl, too young to have figured out these 'universe things'.

"Vedha sir", the utterance brushed against a wound that was just about to heal. It was that one careless touch that stung to rush back the raw, invited memories. The words floated in the air, harmless to anyone except her. She tried to move on, like she had walked towards her bus. But her mind was not on the same page as her body. Sometimes that's how the past resurfaces to tap on our shoulders, unbidden, to just remind us that it was not done yet.

She got stuck for a while, and her mind started to search for him through the window. Her eyes started scanning for him everywhere around the campus, on the pedestrian path, sweeping over all the familiar faces. And then the bike stood, her eyes darted like restless searchlights to find the spot where his bike usually stood, void. There was neither he nor his bike.

But then a thought arose. Just before she had overheard another professor speaking to Vedha over a phone call, which meant he must have either taken a leave for the day or left college earlier. She exhaled, trying to brush off the discomfort crawling under her skin because it was again weird and unfathomable for her, who had convinced herself to move on from, still having the power to shake her so deeply.

"What am I hoping to find in him, that I bother to look for him now?" she asked herself. Resisting herself when her heart had its habits and breaking them was not as easy as deciding to. With the same question whirling in her mind, she reached the room, she drifted into an uneasy sleep and woke up the next morning as if the night had done nothing to erase it. She got ready for college with her mind fixated elsewhere. The moment her bus pulled into the campus, her eyes instinctively looked at the bike stand, relentlessly needing to see him once to confirm his presence or perhaps his absence.

But he was not there at the bike stand. Neither his bike. Despite her scolding, her gaze continued to wander, betraying her heart's quiet rebellion. Saira walked into the class with steady steps and disarrayed thoughts. Anya, who had spent enough time deciphering Saira's silences, caught on to the shift immediately, that there was something unsettled in her eyes that hadn't been there a day before.

"Hey Saira, are you okay?" asked Anya, the ever-observing one.

Saira blinked, snapping out of her thoughts, forcing a smile that could convince the most people, but not Anya and said, "Yeah, I'm fine", one of the most common lies ever.

Anya understood that Saira would speak when she was ready, so she made sure she didn't add on to her battles she couldn't see.

"Why haven't I seen him even once?" This thought was unsettling in her mind.

She had been conscious of his absence since the previous day when she overheard that professor's phone call with Vedha, but now she retraced it to the entire week. So, she tried to recall the last time she had spotted him, which was only the last week when he spoke to her that evening, leaving her with all the clarifications. She felt something was off.

"Anya", whispered Saira.

"Hmm", said Anya, staring at the LCD, which had almost 170 slides. "Vedha hasn't come to college", whispered Saira again.

Anya, instead of whispering and risking the professor's attention, discreetly slid her notebook to Saira with a scribble on the left corner that had the words, "So what", followed by a slightly bigger question mark.

Saira didn't know what to whisper or write back. She hovered over the pen with much deeper meaning than those two words have. It sounded like "Why wanting to rewind?"

She wrote an emoji with a sad face. Anya, gazing at Saira, flipped the page, telling her to turn over her thoughts.

Saira turned upset, and Anya realised this was the thing she had been bothered about since the morning.

Anya whispered, "Are you sure?" "Yeah", Saira humbled her tone.

That was, anyway, not the kind of kiddish friendship. Anya knew very well that Saira held herself accountable for her decisions. Right or wrong, a friend always supports a friend. They don't always agree; they just stand behind, no matter what.

Anya showed her a thumbs-up.

Then in the next interval, they roamed casually on the ground floor, looking for that junior from whom they got information about Vedha previously. She wasn't outside, so they waited for a while and then went into her class searching for her. She was lying with her head down on the desk and woke up on hearing Anya call her out.

"Hi, senior", said that junior girl.

"What's up, what class is now?" asked Anya. "This is a library hour", said that girl.

"Alright, alright, what's the hot news here?" asked Anya casually. "Ah, internals are nearing", lamented that girl.

"Now that's a thought", Anya insisted further.

"Oh, and another one. Vedha sir..." dragged that girl in a sad tone. And that's exactly what Anya and Saira were expecting.

"Vedha sir is leaving the college", continued that girl.

Well, this was a shocker. Unexpected for both Anya and Saira. "Why, you said he is a new one here", asked Anya casually.

"That's right, he is a newbie, but this is not confirmed news yet, as he has been on leave for a week, this information is passed among students, otherwise I'm not sure about it, senior", said that girl.

"Oh, okay", said Anya, looking at Saira.

Then, they both left for their class, leaving a casual bye-bye to that junior girl. Saira and Anya walked back to their class and then, after sitting on their chairs, Anya asked Saira, "So, what now?"

Saira, stuck in her thoughts that weren't voiced, didn't answer immediately. She stared ahead like the answer was written on the air.

And then with a sad tone, she said, "I don't know, I thought I had moved on" Anya paused for a while.

Then came a professor who continued lecturing until the lunch break. But sometimes the real lesson wasn't in the lectures or textbooks. But that was unfolding within Saira's heart. Then came the lunch break. Tearing a small piece of her roti, Anya said, "Look, Saira, I get it. I definitely get it. But, you have to stop standing in the rain, hoping it will turn into sunshine" Saira, twirling her noodles, said, "Maybe I just need a little more time", and shed a drop of a tear.

"Time for what, Saira? To hurt yourself more? To keep reopening the wound?" Anya leaned forward to Saira.

"Anya, I'm still processing a lot, I still don't understand why this has all happened", said Saira, wiping the tears that fell from her right eye.

"I know, right?" exhaled Anya.

"I know it's easier said than to live that", added Anya.

"Anya, I understand you wish well for me to have said this, but honestly, I feel stuck in the mud, unable to either move or progress from this", wept Saira.

Anya placed her palm above Saira's closed fists, and her eyes pointed at Saira's untouched plate. Anya wondered why heartbreak and hunger should mix up, "Some problems in life need overthinking, but we always have the choice to do that with an empty or full stomach. Emotional damage is bad enough, at least we need not add acidity to the list", said Anya.

"Uh-huh", Saira let out a weak chuckle.

They completed their boxes and went back to their classes, and then to their respective nests after another two hours of continuous boring lectures.

Saira sat at her desk with her pen over the papers. That was another assignment nearing its submission deadline, and for once, her mind wasn't lost entirely in thoughts of Vedha. Maybe moved on, but not yet completely. Perhaps that's the art of healing, healing by layers and layers. And then, that night, Saira lay in bed with deeper thoughts and the soft shadows cast by that yellow, dim light against the ceiling fan that ran in slow motion. She knew it was not longing, or not exactly. And not regret as well, she had enough acceptance of the reality. But why did that still bother her? Maybe some emotions don't have closure? Perhaps they just settle within us, becoming a part of who we are growing to be. All these thoughts kept her mind so busy and tiring that she fell asleep off forgetting to switch off the lamp.

It was the next day. Saira did not find Vedha on the bike stand, but there was his bike. She was a little happy inside. And then when she reached her class, she told Anya about this.

"Then, he might have been on leave, I guess, Saira", said Anya. "Should mostly be", agreed Saira.

And then came those slow two hours of staring at the clock in agony. Yes, those lectures.

Saira and Anya were slowly taking steps to the cafeteria to have their lunch, and they noticed an unusual crowd near the admin block. The air around that corridor was hushed with murmurs and curious whispers moving like the air.

"What's happening there?" Anya frowned, shifting her lunch bag to the other hand.

Saira did not care at first until they both got closer. There was Vedha with a backpack and a helmet, surrounded by a bunch of students like buzzing bees.

"Can we check?" Saira nudged.

Anya stood on her toes to find if there was any familiar face in the crowd, and yep, there was her busmate. The junior girl and the informer. She made a hiss of her name and signalled for her to come. Anya, Saira and the junior walked towards each other, and they met.

"What is happening?" asked Anya curiously.

"Senior, the rumour was right, Vedha sir is leaving, it seems. He has given his resignation, but management is negotiating with him, as he was well known for bringing a higher pass percentage in his previous college", said that busmate.

"Oh", Anya controlled her words.

"I don't know, but I heard our dean telling him that they did not just hire him on his approach, they were also seeking some improvements in the college that he is capable of, and the dean said that he did not understand why the enthusiasm in him is lost in a week of joining here, assuring the management would facilitate him more for continuing his job here", added that girl. Anya and Saira looked at each other. They probably knew why they felt uneasy inside.

Saira thought she didn't need his presence, but she realised how much his leave would take a toll on her. She felt like a door slamming shut somewhere deep within. She couldn't hear anything but the rush of her pulse while the voices around her felt distant echoes.

"Saira", Anya held her arms.

They both, along with the junior busmate, moved towards the crowd again. And then they saw each other, Saira and Vedha. The look from Vedha that lasted for a few seconds conveyed the final goodbye to her, and that was one of the painful glares she exchanged with him. She did not stop, she walked along with Anya, crossing and passing over the crowd along with those buzzes in the air till it vanished away, till they reached the cafeteria that was located near the auditorium. Saira tried to compose herself. They both sat with lunch boxes open. But mouths shut.

The day ended with almost no cheer for Saira. She reached her room, refreshed herself, changed into a comfortable outfit, and tied her hair up lazily. The evening stretched like bubble gum that made her feel something amiss. She sat by the window, staring at the dimming sky, the golden hues melted into deep blues like her life lately. She sighed, rubbed her temples, bit her nails and unlocked her phone to see his WhatsApp status. He was online. It triggered her thoughts to speak to him. She held herself back. She wondered if she could talk to him just once, not to rekindle, she knew it was of no use. But just to hear from him.

"Would it hurt or heal?" she asked herself.

She couldn't put her finger on anything, she doubted if she could get a solution from Anya. But then, denied herself what if she just refrained from talking to him? She neither needed that. But it was another hesitation about how she could call a married man at this hour. While she still saw him online, something in her said, maybe he was also waiting for a text or call from her with her chat open, she thought. Well, a woman's intuition is no less sharp than a blade honed by time and experience. She felt in her bones, and there popped up a message from him.

"Good evening".

# DAY 1: One down. How many more?

Her heartbeat rose at how sharp her feeling was, how telepathic it was. Moments like these are where we overcomplicate things, turning our brains into spaghetti, whether it is a sign or test from the universe. Saira glared at the screen with her thumb hovering over her keypad. Those were two simple words that made her mind spin in circles. It's almost a universal experience that when a woman thinks she's moving forward, a curvy smile, a simple message, or a fleeting glance pulls her back into their thoughts. It's a law of nature that a guy somehow finds a way to slip back into a girl's mind, uninvited, like a catchy tune she never meant to hum. And in this case, it was Vedha's action to disappear without information.

She hesitated to reply to him, refraining from breaking a "good girl norm" of not texting a married man. All the boundaries, logic, and self-control crumble when we hit rock bottom because it's in our weakest moments we realise that discipline bows to raw emotion, and the walls we built to protect ourselves often collapse under the weight of our longing, just to realise later that the rock bottom, isn't where we lost ourselves, but where we finally met the parts of ourselves we have been avoiding to heal, to become the best version of ourselves.

The married man tossed another message her way. "Call?"

This time, low-key Saira also wanted to talk to him. His abrupt decision to leave the college puts her in the feeling of losing someone precious, sets her in misfortune and seems unable to reach it any time after it's lost.

She said, "Yes". The only yes she could ever say to him.

In another ten minutes, a call rang with her screen showing Vedha sir, the number she had once saved him as. Now, at this point, it was serving as a reminder for her that he is still, "Vedha sir", for her and nothing more. She swallowed it and picked up the call at almost the last ring when it was about to give up.

"Hello", his voice passed through her eardrums to nerves to brain to gut to everywhere.

Saira, unsure if it was right or wrong, kept her voice intact. It was too late to think of it after impulsively, consciously picking up his call. She fell for this guy, not just with the fleeting glances, but his audacity, his way of respecting a woman's feelings, his grace of honouring what he was bound to. But, wouldn't this call shatter her reasons to have fallen for him?

"Saira", he called upon to break the dead silence.

Saira was still in her thoughts, "What happens to my integrity in talking back to this married man?"

She was worried about what Vedha would think of her now.

"Hello", said Vedha again, bringing back the phone against his face and looking for any signal loss, to then realise it was Saira who was lost.

He waited, and then came a meek voice. "Hello", said Saira.

"Hello", came the voice of Vedha. The fumbling attempts of any lovers with words tripping over themselves often as a dance of hesitation that stretches the silences a little too long, potentially causing overthinking and an adrenaline rush. Besides, these two were tied to a different level of hesitation, giving the prospect of an extra-marital affair to the world. And probably to themselves as well.

"I came to know that you are leaving the college", said Saira with a steady voice.

"Yes", he said. He then paused for a moment and continued, "And I wanted to inform you…that's why I asked for a call".

"Oh", said Saira.

"Hmm, I wasn't sure if I should, but I felt I owed you that much", Vedha dragged.

"But why now, when everything is already settling?" queried Saira. Not just the question she wanted to ask Vedha now, but had been asking herself since she realised his absence from the college.

"Did things settle, Saira? Or just sitting as it is, waiting to be acknowledged?" Vedha asked Saira the question he had been pondering himself, and failed to find the answer.

There existed a moment of silence. "Hello?" asked Vedha.

"Haven't hung up yet", Saira answered to the previous conversation.

"I want you to stay on the line a little longer, too", Vedha dropped a hint.

"Until when?" Saira, with a smirky smile, asked without asking. She caught the clue he let slip from him, but also reminded him that it was not meant to stay.

Vedha couldn't answer this. "Hello", asserted Saira.

There was an instant burst of student chatter in the background with a muffled hum of voices, maybe he walked inside now.

"I'm taking extra hours for my old college students who want to clear their backlogs, every day in the evenings and will reach home after 9 pm, I'm free to talk", said him.

"Ok Vedha sir", Saira reminded him of his reality and hung up at that moment.

And there she sat contemplating. From dusk till dawn, Saira lay awake replaying the entire conversation at least a million times. Sometimes, in life, we cannot comprehend if things happen because we long for some experiences, or we crave such experiences deeply, because some things are destined in our way.

She reprised every word, every pause, and every breath of him. She was feeling on high and was speculating about what falling in love could do to a girl. She wanted to talk to Anya, spilling everything out like the ink on a blank page, but she knew Anya better, that she wasn't the type to let things slide with comforting words. She would question everything, dissect every layer and hold up a mirror to every contradiction Saira was feeling. So, Saira held herself back for now, until she became ready to defend the feelings she badly understood about herself.

So, she chose silence and the shadows over the ceiling from the yellow, dim lamp to be her companion that night.

The next day, Saira reached the college earlier than usual. She went to the cafeteria, which wasn't fully awake, and sat at their usual table. A very few students were scattered around, some flipping through their notes, some with their heads into papers for submitting their assignment by 10 o' clock that day, and some mindlessly scrolling on their phones.

Anya, a certified night owl, was probably waking up, rushing through her morning routine. She never had time for a slow breakfast at home, she would just grab her lunch bag from the kitchen, throw on the first outfit she found and rush out to the college cafeteria for breakfast daily. So, Saira wanted to talk to Anya even before the class started, because she knew she couldn't hold on until there came a break. After all, it was not so straightforward matter to have exchanged one word on their notebook's right corner during the class hours.

Saira exhaled slowly, staring into the distance, hoping Anya would arrive soon.

There came Anya at a distance, parking her black scooter in the student's parking lot and drawing circles in the air with her finger, wreathed with the bike key settled at the bottom. Her eyes widened as she spotted Saira sitting alone at their usual place because it wasn't like her to be here this early, especially in the cafeteria. Anya waved a cheerful "hi" from across the cafeteria with a bright expression of both curiosity and amusement. And then, without breaking her stride, she held up her index finger, signalling one minute before she headed straight to the food counter.

There was the familiar scent of crispy dosa and a mix of chutney and sambar aroma in the air. As she waited, she stole a glance at Saira, noting the distant look in her eyes while her hand rotated on the coffee cup. She smelled something was up. Then, with a plate in hand and the familiar grin, Anya finally made her way to the table, sliding onto the bench across from her friend.

"Alright", Anya said, tearing off a piece of dosa and dipping it into the chutney. "What's the headline, early bird?"

Saira smiled. A smile that had traced the fraction of the same smile as when she blushed on the very first day, when Saira said "An invigilator". Anya understood that there was Vedha in the picture, but wondered why he still existed in the picture, rather than leaving space for her to heal the wounds of fate.

"Him?" asked Anya with a blooming gaze tinged with the softest trace of surprise. "He called me, Anya", Saira paused.

With her three middle fingers touching the palm and only her pinky and thumb extended, Anya raised her hand to her ear in a questioning gesture, meaning, 'over the phone?', while her mouth was busy chewing the bite of dosa.

Saira nodded subtly, swirling the coffee cup.

Anya swallowed and leaned in slightly. "So, you talked?" asked Anya in her casual voice with her eyes that carried the weight of all the questions she couldn't ask her at that moment.

Saira nodded yes again, with her eyes held with a quiet storm of doubt, waiting for a sign from Anya.

"Not a silly move, go ahead", said Anya, wiping the dappled Sambar drop on her lips.

Anya's reply gave Saira the confidence that she could make her understand why she had already spoken to him and still wanted to talk to him.

"He texted me a good evening at first…." started Saira and told the entire conversation of what had happened the previous night.

"So, what have you decided now?" asked Anya to Saira.

"Anya…" dragged Saira, "If you are gonna hate me for this, I would be upset, but this is my genuine feeling from inside, even if it seems or sounds unfair. I couldn't resist this, and I cannot hide or lie to you. I like to talk to him, I wish to share a few nice memories with him, not the memories like usual lovers, we are not, yet, just communicating, sharing each other's views on life and fun and grief, a little more effort to know him as a person. That's all. Not the kind of memories from roaming outside to parks, dashing each other on the beach or in the theatres sipping the same glass of juice with a couple of straws", Saira spoke faster than usual like she had to pour out her heart as instantly as she could so she could get relieved from the weight she has been carrying the last night.

Anya, with calmness, looked at her eyes. She did not say anything back that made Saira doubt her decision. Yet, she waited desperately.

"I will be back", said Anya, standing there with her plate and walking to drop it in the dishwasher corner. Saira waited. Anya came back and took her bag from the bench.

"Come, Saira. We'll talk as we walk to the class", said Anya.

Saira was quite confused about her intentions of delaying her reply, took her bag and walked along with Anya.

"Saira..." started Anya. Saira keenly listened.

"I'm happy for you. I mean, you both need closure, don't you? But that day evening, when Vedha spoke to you or when he tried to leave the college, it looked like a closure, dramatic. But it's an illusion, you still bleed from the inside. And with an open-ended one, you cannot seek closure so that you can move on, is what I felt. You know, sometimes, the only out is 'through'. I vote for your decision", explained Anya.

Saira felt a warmth spread through her chest like a reassurance she needed the most at that moment. They reached their class before the professor came.

"Hey Anya, Hi Saira", their friend from the adjacent bench gave her voice.

Saira smiled and said hi, and Anya acted like a celebrity and made the formal greeting a funny one.

Saira sat in her place, sighed, resting her chin on her hand and said to Anya, "Sometimes it's so hard to choose ourselves, know, Anya? To even think of talking to a married man puts me on the horns of a dilemma. I couldn't give myself any justifications for it, it evokes guilt in me", she uttered in her sombre voice.

Anya kept tapping her pen against the desk, listening to Saira. And then came the professor creaking the classroom door open like the chicken hatching abruptly, unexpectedly from its shell. Some professors function like clockwork, sticking to the routine mechanically, more predictable than a morning alarm. As he came in, he adjusted his glasses, placed a thick bundle of notes on the desk and cleared his throat, preferably the sign he gave everyone to be attentive for the next hour. Then he glanced back at the students to quickly assess the level of attentiveness, inserting his left hand into his pant pocket and a board marker in his right hand and waiting for the low murmurs to settle in.

Anya and Saira knew very well that whispering or using sign language or writing hints on their notebooks was a guaranteed way to land in trouble, a perfect recipe for disaster. So, they remained active and attentive to his class.

"Alright", the professor started.

The lecture rolled on for the next hour like a verbal marathon with no finish line. After half an hour, every minute felt like a test of endurance against drowsiness. Saira was awake, while Anya's eyes turned pinkish, controlling some yawns and hiding a few with her hands casually. Mind drifted, heads bobbed, but the lecture showed no mercy and ended just before the interval time. After the professor took leave, half of the class chose to be drowned in that torpor for another 10 minutes, sleep is precious, they thought. Some wandered with their water bottles inside the class, blinking more than usual per minute, as if trying to wake up, while a few headed to the washrooms, probably for a face wash.

Anya pulled her snack box out from her bag, and there were some grapes her mom had carefully washed and arranged in the small compartment, while the other compartment had some dates and dry nuts. She extended her box to Saira, asking, "How are you still up, Saira? Are you secretly running on caffeine or what?"

Saira chuckled and said, "I don't know I'm immune because I get lost in my thoughts once in 15 minutes", and shrugged.

"Legendary", said Anya, tossing off one almond into her mouth like a pro. "Ah, I don't need snacks, I need some clarity", said Saira breathlessly. "What clarity?" asked Anya.

"On what justifications am I going to give myself for choosing to talk to him now, Anya?", added Saira.

"Why do you need to justify yourself for this, Saira?" asked Anya unpretentiously.

"What? Are you following along? I wonder if you keep pace with my storyline after the lecture", smirked Saira.

"Of course, I'm in", smirked back Anya. "Who else is"? Anya waved her right hand and continued.

"Saira, I'm serious, why should you be feeling guilty about choosing to talk to him?" asked Anya, tossing a grape into her mouth.

Saira wore a sorrowful expression.

"What now? Why are you giving a 'feel sorry for me' kind of look, Saira?" mocked Anya.

"Am I just not talking to someone who belongs to someone else? After all, I have no right to his time, when another woman is sharing his time", asked Saira.

"You nailed a part of it. But the other half needs some tweaking. Yes, someone else is sharing his time. But sharing doesn't mean they belong entirely to them, they just share", said Anya.

Saira was completely baffled by Anya's response. She couldn't find her way out, and that reply had her brain doing somersaults.

"You put me in buffering mode again, Anya", Saira said, scratching her temples. "Okay, listen", started Anya in a serious tone.

"Imagine you are married, would you stop your husband from talking to some random woman he would love to talk to?" asked Anya.

"What?" asked Saira with complete uncertainty. "Just answer me, Saira", insisted Anya.

"Hmmm…." Saira dragged.

Anya waited. "Tell me honestly", said Anya.

"Hmm….it would hurt knowing he chooses someone else's company over mine", Saira answered candidly.

"Uff", Anya pressed her palm against the table with a sigh.

"Then, there is no surprise that you are feeling guilty now", Anya added. Blinked Saira with no clue of what Anya was saying.

"Let me explain", she tossed the last piece of grape into her mouth.

"Most people think love happens just once, and only with one person in their lifetime. If it's so, then it's pathetic how 'love' is given a meaning; it's not love. It's conditioning", sipped an ounce of water, and Anya continued, "Yes, for his good or bad, he married someone else, for this life, and that doesn't mean he cannot have a fleeting glance with you. The problem doesn't exist with the fleeting glance, but with the meaning we associate that fleeting glance with. Until you knew he was married, the fleeting glance felt so divine to you, like a soul wrap. But, why did it change its meaning after you knew he was married?" asked Anya.

It was too much for Saira to process what Anya said. Her lashes trembled as she blinked.

"Were you both in control of what you needed to allow in your lives, when you felt something divinely pulled you both together?" asked Anya.

"No isn't it? Otherwise why would you be stumbling to get rid of his memories now?" asked Anya.

Saira nodded, yet it spoke volumes.

"See, I will talk in terms of your perspective itself. If marriage is so divine, if love should be obstructed and constrained to just one person whom he married, then what you both felt between you, the fate game, the talks he gave on that evening, the heaviness on your heart, are these just your imaginations?", asked Anya.

Saira couldn't swallow, so she couldn't say a word, but the tears, she controlled in her eyes confirmed that what she felt was real.

"Come on! Why would you cry now?" continued Anya.

"Anya and Saira, now it's a lab session, no professor would come", said one of their classmates. Hearing that, Saira and Anya pulled their lab coats from their bag and walked to the lab with their record notebooks and calculators.

Saira was processing a lot inside her mind while also trying to blink away some of the tears that came without her control. Anya casually engaged in chit-chat with her other classmates for a while. She was one of the fancy-free creatures with friends all over the college.

Saira sat with some voltmeters without any force within her to carry out any of her intriguing experiments. "If love happens just once, just with only one person, then it is not love, it's conditioning", these words kept eating Saira.

Anya, who had heard the melancholy that had been played within Saira's heart, came back to her casually.

"Hey", called out Anya. "Hmm", Saira whispered.

"Saira, don't think too much, you need not hold any guilt for talking to him. You have your integrity for life, don't stretch it way too much to normal things like talking to him and feel guilty about it", said Anya.

"Anya...." dragged, Saira and continued, "The only point where I feel unconvincingly guilty is knowing the fact that he would hide my bond with him from his wife", said Saira.

"If he tries to hide, or rigidly hides, that's not just because you both share something that's so not welcomed by society. Maybe he doesn't want to get his life too complicated, maybe not adding fuel to his wife's insecurity issues, maybe for some other reasons too, we don't know. And to think of all that, just gets you looping into this eventually. Just chuck. Be intentional that you talk because you have to get rid of this fate play, you want to add more to it, so that the pain fades away," said Anya.

Saira gave a positive nod, like she understood what Anya told her.

"Just talk. There are possibilities, maybe you like him more, or you start to hate him after getting into talks. Everybody looks inordinately attractive until they open up their mouth and minds. Mostly that's why most couples who seem lovey-dovey while in love, become fighting roosters after marriage," chuckled Anya.

Saira let out a twinkling smile, too.

"I never knew you were this much philosophical on love and relationships", said Saira and smiled.

"Haha, probably why I'm still single", winked Anya. Saira smiled again.

Anya came near to Saira, embracing her with warmth and grounding her at that moment with rare intensity in her eyes with no smirk or playful sarcasm but just with raw concern, and said, "Come out of this trap, Saira", firmly shook her shoulder slightly, as if trying to wake her from a deep sleep and continued, "Play smart. You are not meant to suffer this forever", nodded Anya.

Saira swallowed hard because this was a greater revelation. Sometimes our friends become the voice of reason when our thoughts turn into a tangled mess because they see what we refuse to acknowledge and pull out when we sink too deep, and remind us of our worth when we forget it ourselves. Anya's words truly carried honesty, love and brutal clarity that Saira managed to seek through the cracks of our confusion.

In our lives, there would be 'one moment' of realisation that finally clicks into our mind like a spark that lits the entire system with light. Once we hit that moment, life becomes effortlessly easy in the part, we had been struggling for days, weeks and months, sometimes years too. Life in that segment never feels like a battle anymore. The same challenges exist, the same circumstances, and the same people, but our minds shift, and the way we see things and consume information hits at a different tangent than ever. The struggle wouldn't be fighting against life anymore, but learning to flow with it. With every decision clearer, every minute would feel a little freer. It was one such day for Saira.

She engaged actively in her lab experiments, had fun while eating and endured a couple of more classes. In the evening, Anya and Saira departed from the class, and as they came out of their block, they sighed at each other, probably Saira with a confirmation look of having conceived all the insights Anya gave her, and Anya to wish her a quick recovery and a drift apart. Saira to board her bus, and Anya to the student's parking lot.

Saira sat on her usual window corner; she knew inside that Vedha would come to the parking lot. He came out of his block with his helmet and backpack, which was quite visible from her seat, and she had unhinged thoughts about looking at him now or not. "If there was confusion, it's indeed a no", she thought and leaned back in her seat, giving him outwardly that she did not care to see him by scrolling through her phone.

He saw her at his approach towards the bus and expected her to look at him, but she didn't. He wondered if that was intentional, pretending to be incurious or accidental. With the same doubt, he crossed her bus, picked his bike from the bike stand and went off.

# DAY 2: The kick-off

Saira reached her hostel, got refreshed, had the sandwich and the hostel snack for that day and continued writing in her record notebook. There rang her ringtone. As she peeped, she saw the name "Vedha sir". She thought for a while, but she decided to talk to him anyway. So, she swiped at a 5th ring to answer the call and said, "Hello".

"Hi Saira", said Vedha and continued, "Are you too busy to talk?".

"I was writing my record notebook, but yeah, the deadline is not any time soon, so we can talk Vedha sir", said Saira.

"Okay", acknowledged Vedha and continued, "Well, this is the first time I have heard a sentence this long from you", said Vedha.

"Ah, too much plighted with exchanging glances that never demanded any word", said Saira and smiled with huh voice.

Vedha, who thought Saira was a silent one, was impressed by the actuality and couldn't control his giggle.

"But that moment wasn't a joke", added Vedha. "I know Vedha, sir", said Saira.

"I assumed you to be a silent girl, a much reserved type, but..." said Vedha. "But", interrupted Saira in a friendly tone.

"But, you are not less easy to approach, kind of jovial", said he. "Still, you didn't, Vedha sir", said Saira and shut him.

Vedha felt locked. Saira realised, "Okay, it was neither me too", added Saira.

Vedha's voice shivered a bit, and he controlled it. He said, "I should have, the fault was mine. Mine"

Saira did not want to give space for another melancholy tonight, so she said, "Ok, ok, let's not cry over it again, at least not today, I'm tired, Vedha sir", and chuckled.

"Alright, done", said Vedha.

"So, you are stepping away from the college. Are you sure, Vedha sir?" asked Saira. "Hmm, yeah. Still 5 days more", said Vedha in a neutral tone.

"Just five days?" Saira said to herself.

"But, why? Am I bothering you in any way?" She hesitated, yet asked him.

"Not at all, Saira. It's the other way around. I felt my presence in your life now must be creating unnecessary memories that would grow deeper and unerasable with time and might become hard for you to erase and get rid of. So, I just want to leave you with this level of hurt, I did to you", said Vedha.

Saira's lips parted slightly; she guessed it already, but heard it from him now.

"I guessed, but I have no inconvenience, anyway, we belong to different departments and are never gonna meet to pile up memories anymore that are unpleasant, Vedha Sir. And being in the same college, you are not gonna be my invigilator any more too", Saira smiled, huh, "So you can reconsider working here".

"No, Saira. Living in the same space is gonna keep us reminded that we are punished by life", Vedha exhaled.

"Okay, it's up to you, then", said Saira.

"But, I want us to be in touch in all of these 5 days, Saira. I want to make it the best time of our lives, at least what I can do about it", said Vedha seriously.

Saira was puzzled about what he meant, but still replied, "Ok, Vedha sir," and smiled. "Call me Vedha, isn't it enough?" he asked playfully.

"That's been my way of reminding myself of my boundaries", Saira said in a loving tone.

"Interesting, what can I expect when I make you come out of your boundaries?" asked Vedha playfully.

Saira chuckled aloud and blushed inside.

There was love encircling along with the radio waves of their phones, unseen and undeniable.

A student came to Vedha asking him a question about solving some equations. Vedha told Saira that he would be connecting back to her and hung up.

Saira got back to her record notebook, but now her pen glided mechanically over the pages, just the numbers and the readings copied from her observation notebook.

Her mind was still processing what they had both spoken about over the phone until half an hour before.

As she dropped her pen onto the open notebook, she turned and lay on her bed, staring at the ceiling, her hands resting beneath her head forming a butterfly posture. She liked every conversation she had with him, his voice penetrated through each of her cells, deeper she felt. One hour passed, and she remembered him once telling her that he would be taking extra classes until 9 PM.

The clock was already showing 8 PM, so she decided to complete her dinner before he called, so she could talk and cherish the same time and sleep with it. She rushed to the mess canteen and finished her dinner. She was checking on her phone and was assured its ringtone volume was high, so she wouldn't miss his call in the buzzing chaos in the canteen. Yet, she hasn't received any call from him, even after she returned to her room after finishing her dinner.

As the clock hands moved towards 9, she longed for the minutes to stretch, but they didn't. It became 15 minutes past 9 PM, and there was no call from him, so she made up that he might have returned home. And that was exactly when her phone rang.

She picked at her first ring and waited.

"Sorry, Saira, I was held up with work continuously. I will call you tomorrow evening", he said.

"Oh, alright, thanks for informing", said Saira.

"I knew you would be waiting and so wanted to inform you", he added. Saira smiled and "Ok, bye, carry on", she said and hung up.

Saira realised that the days were slipping through her fingers like sand, and she had less than 5 days to hold onto something that was already slipping away. She wanted to make each moment count with intention. Every glance, every conversation, every shared silence would become a piece of memory she could carry with her.

Thinking of all these moments, Saira slowly lulled into sleep. She drifted into sleep with the conscious thought of him and his voice, their conversations, their pauses and the serenity in them.

# DAY 3: Flower and a Slapshot

The dawn broke with soft golden hues, painting the sky, pushing away the remnants of the night. The world stretched awake, the birds chirping like tiny messengers of a new beginning. Sunlight seeped through the window, touching her face gently, and Saira opened her eyes, blinking away the blur of sleep. The first thing she recollected was that it was one day over and 4 days more.

Saira waited to see him as the bus rolled onto the campus. Vedha was standing there in the bike stand, adjusting his tie with practised ease, rolling down his sleeves and tucking his shirt with an air of effortless nonchalance. His ID card hung loosely around his neck, swaying slightly with his movements. He was turned to the other side, and he did not notice the bus or her. Saira waited to see if he would turn, but the bus passed away while he was absorbed in his world.

But as she got off the bus and walked towards her block, there he was, walking towards her from a distance with his backpack and helmet. He had to cross her block if he started from the bike stand to his block. So, they met face to face as they walked towards each other and they knew to have to cross each other. But that's just when he reached into his pocket and fingers closed around something small. He passed it to Saira's palm as he crossed.

Saira blinked in nervousness. She clutched it tightly in her palm, closing around it as if shielding it from the world. She made it quick that no one seemed to notice, but still, some fear lingered. What if someone had seen it? What if questions followed?

She kept walking, her pace steady, yet a storm brewed inside her. She didn't dare to look back at Vedha, who continued walking towards his block. And then as she reached her block, she found there was none around in the corridor, and as she opened her palm, she found a white little flower that was found in the plants near the entrance, and probably on the way from the bike stand too. She took steps to her class on the first floor, holding it like a secret she wanted to keep to herself. But there was Anya, who had already reached the classroom.

"Hi Saira", Anya, with some other classmates, made a chorus.

"Hi... Hi..." she answered everyone before she came and sat near Anya. "Glow glows everywhere", mocked Anya.

Brows shrank, and Saira looked at Anya and smiled.

"How many hours of endless talk yesterday?" asked Anya. "Just half an hour", said Saira firmly.

"Half an hour? Nah, the glow weighs more", winked Anya.

Saira opened her palm and showed Anya the cute little white flower. The flower was seen everywhere around the college, but never was it this special.

Anya understood that it was about Vedha's gesture and mocked her again, saying, "Hmm hmm, carry on".

Saira smiled with a blush.

Saira did not have any interest in the classes that day; she staredly blinked and blindly nodded her head to the voice of the professor, which sounded like a distant hum to her. She was drowned in those moments when he brushed against her palm with no hurry, no hesitation. It was soft, yet it had sent a shiver down her spine, warmth and chill intertwining like two forces refusing to let go of each other. She swallowed every time she thought of the touch his fingers gave her.

His cute little gesture intensified her anticipation of waiting for his call that evening.

And when we distract ourselves from the classes, the classes run like a marathon and flee away in a minute. Saira already had enough distractions to mentally get lost from the boring lectures, and the evening arrived.

Saira waited in her window corner, and Vedha walked towards the bike stand from his block. She caught his eye that was travelling all along the way to her. She gave back incessant glances, too. The loving gesture conveyed to him how much she liked the cute little thing he did in the morning. He then crossed her bus and headed straight to the bike stand, and kicked the starter to the extra sessions he had been taking.

She reached her room and refreshed quickly while checking her phone once in a while. And there he called.

"Hello", said he.

"Hello", smiled Saira. "Thanks", she added. "For", he asked.

"The flower", she said and blushed and continued, "I was waiting in the morning for you to see, but you were busy tucking your shirt and tie", ended Saira.

"Yeah, like you were busy scrolling your phone before evening", said sarcastically that he knew her intentional pretension that day.

"Oh. Gotcha. So, you knew I was watching over you", she confirmed.

"Otherwise, how would I transfer the flower at the apt timing?" asked him. Blushed she.

"And by the way, how was the flower? I made it simple and small enough to fit between our palms. No hard feelings, okay?" he continued.

"No, no", with a firm denial, "It was the best flower I had ever received, probably the first as well", Saira said, looking at the dull flower that shrieked like a piece of cloth in her palm.

"I will get you a bunch of flowers later", he assured.

Whether it was real or just another fleeting word, it didn't matter now. Saira felt good to hear and said, "Ok, vedha sir", and smiled a huh.

"Call me Vedha, Saira", Vedha stopped.

There was silence. And Saira did not know how to answer him. Vedha continued, "At least for the days left?"

There was still silence, and Vedha held himself back from uttering any more words.

Saira tried to divert by asking her valid doubt she needed to know about his timing for calls, and she asked him, "So, I can call anytime between 6 PM to 9 PM?"

"Yeah", he said in a word.

"So, how old are you? Some 6 to 7 years older than me?" asked Saira casually.

Vedha, although he understood that she was not interested in his request, tried to answer her in his usual way.

"You must be 20 now, right? So, 8 years", replied Vedha. "Oh…" Saira dragged. "8 years!" she repeated.

There was an awkward silence, which both of them tried to cope with. Vedha broke it again. "You are from the IT department, aren't you? So engineering was your passion?" he asked her. "Yes and no", said she tiresomely.

"Yes and no? So why were you here?" asked Vedha,

"I never liked coding, programming and any of the engineering pieces of stuff, I joined in not on my own will. I joined because I had no other choice", lamented she.

"Oops, but you never looked like the one who hated it, at least the sincerity during the exam hall", he complimented her.

"Oh, yeah, I got habituated to pretending or practising to give my best in what I do", said she. Vedha realised the weight underlying her words, but he was redirected by her question.

"You loved engineering?" asked Saira.

"Yeah, I always loved cars, trucks, the way they are designed and functioning, the mechanism, gears and circuits. Engineering sounded so fascinating, and that was why I joined engineering in the first place, but then I ended up with just theories and formulas and exams, which had nothing to do with the things I was passionate about. Instead, I could have joined as an apprentice in a mechanic shop", said Vedha,

It was deep. Saira, who never stood up for herself or her dreams, realised how much he would have buried his passion. But then, the tone of his voice was so funny that she couldn't resist her cute chuckle.

Vedha exhaled and said, "And so cndcd up doing master's and then here as a professor out of some financial constraints".

Saira, being the daughter of a bank manager, never faced any financial crisis in her life. So, she was processing how it would feel to do a job out of basic need or survival.

"Ok, chuck my poor stories, if not engineering, what was your passion?" asked Vedha. Saira's heartbeat rose, her breath stuck, and her chest filled with heaviness all of a sudden.

She exhaled with no strength to voice her thoughts, and weakly whispered, "No, I don't think my passion is possible", said Saira.

"Hmm, I wonder what kind of passion it must be. Formula 1 race car driving?" he asked in a fun tone.

Saira was silent, and he sensed some sadness in it.

"Ok, ok, if you have any financial constraints, I will help you with it any time, Saira. Well, not just financial constraints, you can share any constraints you have about it", affirmed Vedha.

"Particularly financial, because I knew how it hurts to run behind money while also carrying a whole lot of fire inside the heart", he tediously said.

The conversation took a deeper turn abruptly that weighing upon each other's chests.

Realising it, Saira asked, "If at all you had money, you would have carried your passion, isn't Vedha, sir?

"I know, I could have, but I have come a long way now that my priorities just keep my passion away, but for you, I'm not telling it for just the sake of saying it, Saira, and you know it", said Vedha firmly.

"Cool, Vedha sir, I know! I was kidding you", admitted Saira.

"But you haven't become too old to re-dust your dumped passion, it's a reminder from me", added Saira.

"Yeah, a reminder from my feeble granny who failed to follow her passion due to misfortune, thank you, granny", he made fun.

Saira chuckled, and then he hung up, saying he would call after 9 PM for a good night.

Saira then had dinner and came back, lay on her bed. She knew Vedha had kindled some deep- seated beliefs and fears she had about following her passion. "I wonder what kind of passion it must be. Formula 1 race car driving?" his voice kept replaying in her mind like the stuck old tape recorder. It was like a slapshot to her, making her realise that her passion was not just as tough as car racing. Maybe, tough in the literal sense of deciding and gearing into her dream, but she better understood that her dreams never had any external limitations that stopped her from pursuing what she dreamt of. Not needing coaching to pursue a car racing passion, not needing financial means to bring that to reality. Nothing. This realisation hadn't come to her in all of these years. It hit her deeply with his voice, "I wonder what kind of passion it must be. Formula 1 race car driving?" perpetually over the night that she slept out of tiredness.

# DAY 4: A dinner date

One more time, dawn shattered the darkness, bringing a rare sense of clarity to Saira. She felt fresh. She felt loved because of Vedha's little gestures. She felt the meaning of dragging herself to the college was unlikely. As the sky brightened, so did her stillness in mind and calmness in her aura. She arrived at her bus stop and then at college. She looked for Vedha in the bike stand and found only his bike, meaning he had come to college. Her mind thought of the possibility of him crossing her while walking towards the block, her eyes searched for him all over the place, but he wasn't coming from anywhere. With a deceitful face, Saira reached her class and sat straight away in her place with her bag on her lap.

"Hi, madam", a voice popped up, and it was Anya. "Hi Anya", said Saira.

They never needed to compulsively fill the gaps that existed without any topic to discuss. A rare friendship.

The classes went on and on until students finally gave up just before their lunch break.

Saira's phone vibrated with a notification in the name, "Vedha Sir". It was visible to Anya, and she noticed it before Saira turned to her phone.

Anya cleared her throat, sarcastically picking a spoonful of vegetable salad. Saira and Anya were smiling seeing each other.

"I don't mind", said Anya.

Saira smiled at Anya and opened the message that said,

"Another professor was accompanying me, I had to head to my block, I will call by the evening".

Most women don't desire big things in life. Generally, these small gestures of valuing their time and presence are enough, which most men do not understand. She felt appreciated and replied "Ok Vedha Sir" to the message.

Saira waited for the evening, while the professors warned about their exams approaching at the end of the coming month and practical exams being scheduled before their semester exams, holding very less study holidays that semester. Saira noted all the instructions, but her priorities and interests were utterly on spending the last three days with Vedha, who was gonna quit his job at her college.

Then the evening came, and she occupied her usual window corner to easily glance at him from a distance at the bike stand. But another professor accompanied him as he walked along. Saira did not want to get caught or even give the smell of something happening between them. So, as she saw, she casually scrolled her phone. Yet, unsure if he crossed over or not, she looked up and there, he was nearing her bus and talking to his colleague, and still winked at her.

It felt heroic, her heart raced up like it had run a marathon a moment ago. It felt different and nice, but ensured that no one saw her at that moment. She was flying high from inside, and the pace of her bus was least matched. She felt she could live her entire life reliving the moments when she received a flower from him and then a wink from him. It felt so complete that she had lived over 1000 years with him. She was assuring herself that she decided to talk to him because this experience she had was something that she never anticipated before taking that first step.

She waited for his call, with a fruit bowl on her table and phone in her hand. She waited for an hour, and when it was 7.30 PM, she was done waiting and she called him, although she knew he might be busy teaching something there. It rang completely, but he did not pick up. She waited for a couple of minutes before she could try the next time, but he called back before that. She picked at his first ring and said, "Hello, is everything okay?"

"Hmm, sort of. Saira, I'm busy right now, but can you do me a favour?" asked Vedha. "Don't have dinner. We will go out tonight", said Vedha.

"What?" Saira expressed her shock.

"Why? Won't you come out with me, Saira?" asked Vedha. "Noo, it was not about that", murmured Saira.

"Then what?" asked Vedha.

"Come with me if you trust me", said Vedha.

"Okay, at what time?" asked Saira, thinking about what she had to tell her warden, who would communicate everything to her dad.

"Between 8.30 to 9 tonight", said he. "Okay", said Saira before she hung up.

Saira was tense about how to manage things to conceal it from her warden and then eventually her parents. She gave a lot of thought and ended up, she couldn't hide and drafted a plan quickly. She called her dad, her hand shivering, but managed her voice, "Daddy, my friends are going out for dinner tonight. They want me to join them, and me too. Can I go and come back to the hostel?" lied mercilessly.

And that's how lies gradually become a part of love life. "Oh, why suddenly?" questioned Dad.

"It was in the plans, I told them I wouldn't make it before, but as the day approached, I was wished by them and I felt like spending some time outside the hostel, having some different food too, daddy", she lied again.

Food is the emotion for all daddies, especially when it comes to their children. He was touched. He permitted her to go. It felt like a wine, and she was both nervous and excited about her first outing with her 'love', Vedha. While she was getting ready, the phone rang. She thought it was Vedha, but it was Anya.

Saira was shaking again. Now, she would manage her daddy who is far apart, but how to manage Anya who knows everything about her. Could she tell her the truth? But she promised her that she would just talk to him.

And Anya agreed on the same terms that 'just talking' isn't a sin for life. Now, in what ways could she explain this sudden outing plan? She said okay, too? Saira went into anxious mode. But, swiped to attend the call.

"Where are you, Saira?" asked Anya.

This question from Anya is out of sync. Saira was doubtful but replied casually, "In my room, Anya".

"I mean…where are you going?" asked Anya.

"Is she a foreseer or what?" wondered Saira and dragged, "Anyaa…." "Your dad called me and told me safe supper", interrupted Anya.

That was bomb-dropping to Saira to realise that his daddy cross-checked the information with her friend.

"Oops", said Saira.

"Nothing to worry, I told him that I would drop you at your hostel once we are done, but now tell me, where are you going, it must be Vedha, right?" Anya hit the nail.

Saira was relieved for a moment that Anya managed to get to her dad. Escaped. But then Anya hit her straight to the point. What could she possibly say to her when she is doubtful about something in its righteousness?

"Anya, he asked me if I could have dinner with him tonight. I will return to my room after dinner ", she said in a steady, low voice.

"Okay, call me if I have to pick you up and drop you at your hostel and also leave me a message when you reach your room", said Anya, understanding that Saira was unsure of her decision, but still she stood for her.

Saira was relieved by half, at least she was not hiding from her friend and felt validated for being true. "Sure, Anya, thanks for understanding", said Saira.

"Come on, Saira!" cheered Anya and hung up.

It was already 8 PM and she had to start in another half an hour. She stood before her wardrobe with her fingers brushing against the fabric of each dress, unsure of what to wear. She had never been to a dinner date like this before and never had to chance to think about the dress codes for a date. Yet again, was it a date? They were just going to talk.

Still, even talking or eating together was going to be a special occasion, because she didn't have time with Vedha, the first ever person she fell head over heels for. So, she wanted to choose a night she would remember long after it ended. She wondered if she could choose a stylish jumpsuit or an elegant dress with minimal jewellery, or she could wear a flowy maxi dress, which she had never had a chance to wear to college. And then immediately stuck a thought, "Oh, I'm still not in the right to date this guy, although we both like each other". She stumbled and chose her regular kurti with a chinos bottom and the usual sandal she would wear to college. And she was nervous, unlike the other evening when she agreed to Vedha's request for a 15- minute talk. She checked for the cash in her wallet, her phone with some decent charge to reach back hostel without it going dead. And then she sat quietly on a corner of her bed holding the wallet and phone in one hand, correcting those loose strands of hair that fluttered in the fan's breeze.

She was wondering in imagination how his presence felt in her proximity. When he glances from a distance, her heart beats faster, and her breath skips sometimes. She felt chills inside but still sweated outside despite the breezy, cool air from the ceiling fan. And then came the call from him. She swiped in the first ring. "Hello", she whispered in a soft voice.

"Saira, are you ready?" Can you walk out of the hostel and take the right from the college bus stop?" asked him ardently.

Stuck with the confusion of what was reality and what was imagination, she answered, "Ah ah, Okay, I will come", said Saira and hung up.

Vedha still wanted her to be on the line until she reached him. But he understood her sense of nervousness and waited. Saira locked her room, went down the stairs and went near the reception to inform the warden before leaving. But when wasn't he on the chair? While Saira searched for the warden, a lady peeped from the guest room and said, "Saira, carry on, your dad has spoken already"

"Okay, ma'am", she replied, but got more tense about hiding this from the dad who has informers all over the place. She, anyway, had Anya by her side, but the warden could never be for her. Eventually, her thoughts again shifted to what was being more right and wrong. And yet, walked out of the hostel. She walked to the bus stop, 500 meters away. She had never seen it in the dark, this was her first time since she joined this engineering college and the associated hostel. She had no time to explore what was happening around her and walked straight to the bus stop and took her right turn as Vedha instructed. She walked into that street and simultaneously searched for him, recollecting what shirt he had been wearing that day. It didn't hit her senses until she realised she hadn't seen him in the morning and evening when he came along with another professor, 'his wink', mesmerised her, and she failed to recall his shirt. While processing all these in mind, she walked quite a decent distance, yet did not find him.

As she realised, it was entirely dark, no shops were there, houses and no people either. She got scared out of nowhere, and she decided to call him. She unlocked her phone and swiped a call, and she heard a ringtone. As she turned, there he was, standing behind her with his regular smile. Her heart beat faster. It was him. He was so casual, but she was all anxious, previously about hiding the very first thing from her dad, and then on getting lost in the night, and now seeing him in her utmost proximity, especially at a dinner date.

She stood still, like rooted to the spot, paralysed. "Oi", he waved his hand over her face and smiled.

"Hold up a little while walking, you are switching gears and never applying brakes", he mocked her in his love language and laughed. He did not laugh at his joke, but he was over-enthusiastic to see her girl come for him at this late evening.

Saira had to shake herself a hundred times to make herself believe it was all real. Yet, she behaved and tried to accommodate herself in the situation. She smiled at Vedha softly.

"I was afraid if I missed the path", said she.

"I never guide the wrong route to those who trusted me, at least, I keep them from harm", he said back.

Saira couldn't blink; she almost drifted into a dream-like state. "Hello", "Excuse me", he said.

"Ah", she said as she woke from her imagination.

"I'm so hungry, can we walk to the restaurant?" he asked. "Yeah, okay okay", she said and walked alongside him.

"Saira, look there!" Vedha pointed out the shadow cast upon the dim street light that had a young man and a girl walking at his side.

Saira looked there, felt beautiful, flying from inside and then with a smile, she looked into his eyes. The eyes that once showed her a different realm she had never experienced. The same eyes, she never recovered from her fall. But today, it was less effective, as his entire face smiled with charm. It was very evident to her how much he was joyous that evening. It deliberately and contingently explained to her how much she meant to him. Her half-confusion vanished away in that evening breeze as she felt the genuineness of his wholesome smile. They both walked, enjoying the moving shadow that came along with them, until there came another bright lamplight at the street corner. There was a restaurant with a moderately fuzzy chaos of humans wandering here and there in that buffet. Vedha had already booked a couple of seats in the premium lounge with a traditional serving. The bellboy opened the door as they walked in, and the bearer came as they sat in the chairs facing each other.

"What would you love to have?" asked Vedha.

"Anything is fine", said Saira as she already had enough for the day. "Your smile fulfilled my soul tonight", Saira said to herself.

"I will call after deciding", said Vedha to the bearer. Then the bearer left from there and stood at a distance where he could be called with ease.

"You are a vegetarian or non-vegetarian?" asked Saira of Vedha. "Both", said Vedha and smiled. Saira smiled back with a huh.

"This restaurant is famous for the curries they make, so let's order some tortilla or chapati or butter naan and eat with gravies, is it okay for you?" asked him.

"Your wish is mine", she said softly.

"Come on! I want you to have nice food that sticks in your tongue for long", insisted he. "Ok, will go with butter naan", she said, "Curry, I'm not sure, you decide on"

"Okay", said Vedha, understanding her. He looked at the catalogue for a while and called the bearer.

"One fish curry, one chicken tikka masala and two butter naan", said Vedha. Turned to Saira, "Okay?" he checked on her.

She nodded, and he signalled "done" to the bearer.

"You have already been to this restaurant", asked Saira to fill the space.

"No, this is my first time, but I did some research to find the best out here", said he while turning the glass upside down and filling water into it.

"Have some water", he extended the glass to Saira. Saira grabbed it gently and had a sip.

"This is my first time", said Saira.

"This restaurant", he pointed down his index finger and signalled.

"For the restaurant, for the dinner outside of the hostel", she sighed "First time without my friend Anya, and first time after lying to my dad", she sighed at the doorway.

Vedha realised how much she valued him and said, "Thank you, Saira". Saira smiled.

"And did your friend know that we are meeting tonight, I had to plead with her to talk to you for just 15 minutes that day….uff", exhaled.

"Yeah, she knows", said Saira with her head bent down.

"But she is a wonderful friend to you, Saira. I haven't seen such friendship among girls", said. "Yet, didn't she stop you from meeting me?" added.

"She is a good friend who offers me love and truth without sugarcoating, but never without warmth. I always have a mix of admiration and gratitude for her, she is the one who helped me navigate my hostel life and engineering life, and make it not too bad", Saira said from her heart.

They received the ordered food on their table. Vedha stopped the bearer who was about to serve and signalled to him that he would take care of the rest. Saira watched as Vedha carefully placed the butter naan on her plate. The golden layers glistened under the warm restaurant lights and the melted butter pooling at the edges.

For a moment, it wasn't just food. It manifested a quiet gesture of care and tenderness that words couldn't hold. She felt her heart tighten and truly lived the moment.

"Thank you", she said softly with her fingers brushing against the warm naan as she tore a piece. Vedha did not reply immediately; he simply served himself, as if this was the most natural thing to do. But, Saira knew, this wasn't just about sharing the meal; this was about sharing the moment. Saira chewed her piece of naan slowly, her mind drifting between the warmth of the food and the weight of the moment. The restaurant buzzed softly in the background, clinking plates and murmured conversations and the occasional burst of laughter from another table. But here at their table, time felt like it had stilled. Vedha dipped a piece of naan into the fish curry with unhurried movements.

"You know", he started, without looking up, "I never imagined sitting like this with you". Saira, with her piece stuck between her fingers, was spilt with a teardrop she shed.

She blinked fast and pulled the tissues from the table, and blotted her tears. She then lifted her gaze, "Why?" she asked.

Vedha smiled faintly, like he was caught in thought, and he wasn't sure he should say it out loud.

"Because…." he dragged, "some things in life aren't meant to happen, no matter how much you wish they would", he said.

Saira swallowed. There it was, the unspoken reality between them. A truth neither of them dared to name. "But it did happen today", she said with her voice quieter now, "At least, for this moment".

Vedha looked at her. The dim lighting reflected in his eyes, making them softer than she had ever seen before. "Yes", he admitted. "For this moment", he added.

The silence ruled the next 15 minutes as they enjoyed each other's companionship that night. It wasn't an awkward silence, it was neither empty nor unsaid, but a kind of acknowledgement of what they meant to each other. There was no rush to fill the moment with unnecessary conversations. They had an understanding that whatever this was, whatever they were, it did not need descriptions and subtitles.

They completed their shared meal, moment and a few words of exchange. Saira walked to the washroom. Her mind was a mix of emotions, gratitude for the moment and a kind of fulfilment. She took a deep breath as the cool water ran over her hands. She stared at the reflection in the mirror. As she approached the table, she noticed Vedha was already standing, slipping his wallet back into his pocket. The bill had been paid.

"You didn't have to", she said softly, tilting her head.

Vedha smiled with his usual composed expression in place, "I wanted to", he said. "Chivalry isn't dead, after all", Saira chuckled.

He winked and picked up his keys from the table and looked at her. "Shall we?"

She nodded, adjusting her bag on her shoulder. As they walked out of the restaurant, the night air greeted them with a gentle breeze, it was already 9.30 PM. The city lights flickered at a distance. Neither of them spoke as they reached the parking lot. They both knew this night would end soon, yet neither wanted to acknowledge it.

"Thank you for the dinner", said Saira, breaking the silence.

Vedha turned to look at her, something unreadable in his gaze. "Thank you for coming", he said.

"This night couldn't end much better", Saira smiled. They walked slowly, and as the hostel gates came into view, Saira slowed her steps, feeling the weight of the night settle in. She turned to Vedha and, with her voice softer than usual, "Will see you tomorrow", she said.

Vedha gave a small nod, his eyes lingering on her for a moment longer than necessary. "Yeah, see you", he said.

As she walked towards her hostel, Vedha waited at the same place, wanting to exchange a last glance with her before she entered the reception of her hostel. And there he got it and gestured a good night from that distance. Saira gave a final look and went directly to the reception table to fill in and out timings in the register notebook and informed the warden that she was back.

She then unlocked her room, switched on the fan, called her dad and informed him that she had reached the room. He then queried for five more minutes about the food she had and friends she met, which somehow she managed to lie about it and hung up.

Then the message she felt obliged to. A "reached" message to Anya. As soon as she sent it, there came an instant "Ok" and "Sleep well" from her as if she had waited for the confirmation. Whatever had happened that day, from his cute little secret wink to the delicious unforgettable dinner, was overwhelming, dumping happiness and satiation into her that she was extremely tired. Of course, appended are those lies to her dad that made her extra anxious. So, she had no energy left to refresh and sleep; she lay on the bed and fell asleep.

# DAY 5: Lost hours

It was yet another beautiful morning, as Saira had slept early the previous night, and she had woken up an hour earlier than usual. As she opened her eyes after a long, continuous, uninterrupted, full-fledged sleep, she wondered if all these were happening in real life. She saw herself in the same attire as she was in last night's dinner. She squished the pillow that was aside and cherished the moments she had yesterday during her dinner date, and then she resisted getting up from her bed and lay for another half an hour, before bringing herself the regular morning routine.

And then popped a message from Anya as she locked her room to leave the hostel. "I'm waiting in the college cafeteria".

"Ok", Saira replied to her and boarded the bus. The rumbling wheels stilled as the bus found its regular stop within the college grounds. Saira stepped down and walked straight to the cafeteria. Anya's bag was found in their usual place, but Anya wasn't. Saira looked out for her, and there came Anya with two hot coffees in each of her hands and set them on the table, one for her and another for Saira.

"Thank you, I needed a coffee", said Saira.

"I know", Anya assured and continued, "So, how was last night?" raising an eyebrow as she adjusted herself in the seat. Saira stared somewhere away from her and said, "It was nice", with her voice neutral. Anya smirked, nudging her playfully, "Nice? That's all I get? You went out for dinner with your Vedha, sir, not for a lecture on fluid mechanics".

Saira felt relaxed with her funny tone and did not control her small chuckle. However, she did not reply immediately. She wasn't sure how to put into words what last night had felt like, Anya waited taking two more sips of her coffee and then Saira said, "Anya, he was so kind. Moreover, he was so happy, his entire face was hidden beneath his glowing smile", Saira's face bloomed as she said it.

Anya was intrigued to hear more from her. She made complete eye contact with Saira while also sipping her coffee.

"He ordered food, asking for my favourite food, he served me, stopping the bearer, he ensured I was comfortable, and he was surely the safest place for any woman", Saira felt as she said.

"Oh", exclaimed Anya. "And what did he say?" added she.

"Hmm..." she dragged as she thought. "He said he never thought this moment would happen in his life, he said he was so happy about it", said Saira.

"And", Anya insisted.

"And? That's all. He walked with me until he saw my hostel gates, and then we drifted apart to each other's place", said Saira.

"Seriously?" asked Anya.

"Yeah", Saira gave a genuine smile. "We did not talk a word until we ate the full plate, probably he also loved that silence that existed between the breaths we shared in the proximity".

"Ok, ok, have your coffee", Anya pointed at her cup.

As they finished and walked towards their class, Anya draped her arm over her shoulders and said, "Saira, it's all fine until now. But, please consider meeting him alone in public places. What if someone sees you both?" suggested Anya.

Saira sighed adjusting the strand of her that flew on her forehead, "I know Anya, I have thought about it too. Yesterday was so impromptu that I couldn't resist him saying no, but the hesitation I had just flown off the moment I saw his face glooming on seeing me", said Saira.

"Hmm..hmm is it?", mocked Anya and continued, "I knew you both were just talking, but it's about how people perceive a girl spotted with a married man, and you don't want that kind of trouble, trust me."

"Yeah, I hear you, I will be careful", assured Saira.

Anya gave her a knowing look. "Being careful is one thing, drawing a line is another? Just think about it, okay?"

Saira nodded, but deep inside, she wasn't sure if she wanted to stop. Yet, she kept thinking about what Anya said.

"Was the food tasty?" diverted Anya.

"Far better than my hostel mess food", smirked Saira.

They both reached their class, and it was over with hectic amounts of new concepts being lectured on. It was another day of overload for engineering students. While Vedha was also stuck in an unplanned meeting in the evening, Saira found only his bike in the stand, but had no hints of his presence anywhere. She searched for him until the bus started from the college. And reached her room, without seeing him for the entire day.

Saira sat on the edge of her bed, running a towel through her damp hair. The soft hum of the ceiling fan filled the quiet room as she checked her phone screen for the third time in the last two minutes, just to see no notifications. No missed calls.

She sighed, placing her phone beside her. "Maybe he wouldn't call tonight, maybe they needed to stop meeting like this, stop talking like this", she thought. Just as she leaned back against the pillow, the phone screen lit up.

"Vedha Sir".

She took a second to steady herself before answering, trying not to sound too eager. "Hello", she said softly.

"Oi", he spilt his enthusiasm.

It felt good to her. Yet, she was caught between what Anya said in the morning and Vedha's last few days.

"Why so faint?" queried him, catching her low energy levels. "No, nothing", Saira confirmed.

"Quite engaged all day, Saira. Feeling extremely tired like its Friday. Yet it is only Wednesday", he took a long exhale.

"Yeah, I feel like it, too. And I guessed probably that was why we didn't see each other today", added Saira.

"Huh, yeah, there was another negotiation that happened in the evening today", said Vedha. "To withdraw your resignation?" asked Saira.

"Yeah", said Vedha.

"Oh okay", Saira dragged, thinking she would have to make her mind up because she could not force his decision to leave, without knowing what was exactly going through his mind. She felt, she assured him of not disturbing him, and so remained silent.

"Thank you, Saira", started Vedha. Saira paused, wondering why a thank you would erupt now. He continued, "Yesterday night, I dozed off effortlessly, drifting off into the most restful sleep I had been longing for. You were the reason for it. Thank you for trusting me and for the dinner eventually."

"I collapsed into bed and slept without a care in the world, too. A night of true rest after what felt like an eternity", added Saira.

"I had never been as happy as I was yesterday, maybe it was what falling in love feels like or what, I'm not able to figure out", said Vedha.

Saira smiled humbly with little traces of blush.

"I wish it all happened", Saira couldn't resist telling this.

Vedha paused without having any control over what had happened. Saira then felt she shouldn't have said this.

"Ok, what do you want to be, Saira? Do not tell me an Engineer. I knew you didn't like it. I ask for what you wish you to be. Not what your dad wants you to be", asked Vedha.

Saira let out a soft chuckle, one that held no humour, maybe pain. "Ah, we are talking about something impossible. If it was meant to happen, I would not have been given this life. I know I'm so unlucky", she exuded back to a sombre mood.

Vedha leaned back in his chair, staring at the distant wall and fingers drumming lightly on the surface of his desk, he felt as if his attempt to cheer up again from the unfulfilled love had failed. Yet, he continued, "Saira, that's where you are wrong. Nothing in life is set in stone. We shape our own paths, sometimes we just need the courage to take the first step".

Saira sighed, turning onto her side and resting her head on her palm. "Oh really, that was why we did not mean to end up together", asked, seeming to be wrapped in sadness.

"I would say yes. We did not try, and time fleeted, that we missed each other", said Vedha. Saira did not utter a single word.

"Can you deny it now, come on, and tell me", said Vedha.

Saira scoffed. "But, still, it's impossible. I had already tried for it. It is not as easy as you think, let's leave my dream. Why didn't you try yours?"

"You never say it otherwise", smirked Vedha on her for not revealing her true passion was for and continued, "You know, Saira, if life had gone my way, I wouldn't be in this shirt and tie, pretending to be a professor unwillingly abiding by the management rules and be strict to students. I would have my mechanic shop initially and then a firm- the one where I design and build automobiles from scratch", said Vedha.

Saira tilted her head, intrigued, "Wow, that sounds awesome".

"Yeah, I have always loved machines, taking them apart, understanding how they work and putting them back together better than before. That's what was real engineering to me, not the equations in a textbook but the grease and the gears, the sound of an engine coming to life", exhaled Vedha.

Saira admired his love for his passion.

"Hmm, that sounds perfect for you, but why didn't you pursue it?" queried Saira. He chuckled, "Easier said than done. Life isn't always that simple, Saira".

"But you just said we shape our own paths", she challenged. "What if this isn't the end of your dream? What if it's just waiting for you to choose it?"

Vedha stared at the same distant wall for a moment, her words hitting deeper than expected. He said, "You got me now, I have to admit that was kinda cute. Should I pretend to be upset now?" Vedha chuckled.

"No, Vedha sir, that was not my intention" Saira turned serious. "Ok, ok, chill", said Vedha.

Saira's voice carried a mix of frustration and a sense of withdrawal as she shared her thoughts with Vedha. "You know, I have always felt it's easier for a man to pursue his passions. He doesn't need to ask anyone for permission, unlike us girls, who first depend on our daddies and then sugar daddies. Maybe financial independence would help some, but women don't always have their will to operate easily, unlike men."

Vedha's brow furrowed, sensing the weight behind her words. "Saira, I understand the heaviness behind your words. But society has unfair expectations of men, too. Men, being the breadwinners, always had their compulsive need to bear the financial burden on their shoulders, creating only fears and discouragement, even if they have passions."

"Okay, not all men, maybe. At least my dad has no financial constraints. It was just about expectations in my case. I'm just bouncing as a ball between the constant need for approvals, the fear of judgment and the limitations imposed. I have nothing else better to add to it", smirked Saira.

Vedha reached out gently, placing his hand on the side wall. "I can't pretend to fully grasp your experience, but I want you to know that your passions are valid. You deserve to pursue them without seeking anyone's permission."

A faint smile tugged at Saira's lips.

As a couple of students approached Vedha with their textbooks clutched tightly, their eyes filled with curiosity. Vedha turned to them with a warm smile. He said to Saira, "I will be back," and hung up as she said, "Ok"

Saira lay on her bed, staring at the ceiling, but instead of the breeze sound, all she could hear were the recent conversations that echoed in her mind. The clock on her wall read 8 PM, and yet, her phone remained silent. No call or message from him.

A part of her had expected this, but another part, one she hated to acknowledge, had hoped otherwise. She sighed, pushing aside the restless feeling in her chest and got up. Maybe some food would distract her.

She headed downstairs to the mess, the yellow dim lights casting shadows as she picked at her dinner without much appetite. The chatter around her felt distant, like background noise in a life she wasn't fully present in the moment. She was indulged in much deeper prospects of what they had just discussed. She also kept checking her phone often for any calls from him. By the time she returned to her room, it was past 9 PM. She sat on the edge of her bed with her phone resting beside her as if staring at it long enough would make it ring. She checked it once, twice. Nothing.

9.15 PM

9.30 PM.

Still nothing.

She exhaled slowly, pressing her lips together, forcing her to accept the obvious, despite her wishes and desires, one more time. He had probably gone home, or maybe he was exhausted, maybe he needed some space or maybe simply he had nothing to say for now. Whatever the reason, she made up her mind that she wouldn't call. She wouldn't disturb him. "If he wanted to talk, he would", she thought.

Saira brushed her teeth, the minty freshness doing little to wash away her lingering need for him to call and talk to her. She moved through the motions. Rinsing, wiping her face, and tidying up her bed as if keeping busy would stop her thoughts from drifting back to him. But, no matter how much she tried to distract herself, her eyes kept flickering toward her phone.

She adjusted her pillow, set her blanket neatly and turned off the bright overhead light, leaving only the soft glow of her bedside lamp. The night outside was calm except for the occasional rustling of leaves. Letting out a deep sigh, she plugged in her earphones and scrolled through her playlist, searching for something to fill the silence. She tapped to play a song close to her heart, one that held memories of comfort and nostalgia. As the melody wrapped around her, she closed her eyes, allowing herself to sink into the music.

As time went on, the song drew her further into a realm of memories and untold aspirations. The song's melody surrounded her like a gentle whisper, and before she knew it, her mind started to create a fantasy where she and Vedha were together, impervious to the severity of the outside world and simply living inside the lyrics of the song. She imagined them walking together on a calm street, the evening wind blowing through her hair while he looked at her with the same, unfathomable look. She imagined his palm brushing across hers, timid yet warm as though he were trying to probe a line none of them prepared to cross. She pictured a world where he never had to walk away, and she never had to pretend losing him didn't feel like losing a part of herself.

The song held her deeper as they sat together under a starlit sky, his voice low, filled with stories he only shared with her. She could almost hear the way he would laugh at her silly thoughts, how he would fall into moments of comfortable silence, both of them knowing they did not need words to understand each other. But then, as the final notes faded, the reality came crashing back. Maybe this was all they would ever be, the fragments of a dream that only existed when the music played. She opened her eyes, blinking at the glow of her phone showing a call from "Vedha sir".

She couldn't believe it because it was already 11 PM, and he would be at his home. So, wondering why he would call her then, she swiped right to answer the call with both confusion and excitement.

"Oi", he affectionately called her in the way only he could.

"Hi", softly whispered Saira with a shilly-shally of not knowing the possibility of a married man calling her at 11 PM.

"What's keeping you busy at this hour? I thought you would be dozing off by this time, but you are surprisingly picking up my call at the very first ring", he exclaimed.

"Sleep refused to show up tonight, and I let the music take over it. Wait, what is this unusual time you are calling me?" queried Saira.

"Why? Is it not okay for me to talk to you tonight? Am I not supposed to?" he asked. "Oh, not at all, I was asking about your situation", murmured Saira.

"Yeah, nobody is at home, and I thought I could talk to you", he said.

"Ok fine", Saira replied with no interest in asking more about it. Not because she did not care or disliked to talk about but to not place him in any inconvenience.

"Hmmm…" he exhaled deeply, showing great relief from stretching his body. "What's up, Vedha sir?" asked Saira.

"You have got to tell me", he said. The usual sweet nothings between lovers. "Hmmm", they both hummed together.

They laughed at each other's timing.

"Okay, what had we spoken about in the evening?" asked Saira.

"We spoke, yeah, about your passions, but you never revealed it until we hung up", smirked Vedha.

"Oh, right. I have got something to tell now", Saira brought the liveliness. "Yes, I would love that", intrigued Vedha.

"Okay, that's just my suggestion. Setting up a centre for designing on your own is your biggest concern, right?" confirmed Saira.

"Yeah, one of the reasons. I don't want to start something and struggle to keep running it", assured him.

"You, anyway, own much fondness from your 'fan' students, know?" said Saira. "Oh really?" Vedha chuckled.

"Come on, not a situation to show your humility, Mister Vedha" Saira cut him off and continued.

"You are already surrounded by students who admire you. Why not involve them? You can train them, and let them work in your shop as interns- at least in the beginning. They will get hands-on experience, and you won't have to worry about paying them right away. It will still be a win-win for those who are passionate about machines like you", Saira conveyed.

"So, you mean, I can continue teaching at college and after hours, I run the garage with students alongside working with me?" confirmed Vedha.

"Exactly", she said, feeling a rush of excitement. "You possibly can choose studious boarding students, because they neither don't like to be in the hostel nor want to roam outside like the backbenchers, but for sure this will keep them in their interest. This way, you will have a steady income from your job, and at the same time, you will build your shop without financial pressure. More than that, your students will gain real-world experience. Imagine when they are not complaining about engineering as just equations and derivation, unlike you, when they complete engineering. Eventually, as you get clients and business picks up, you can start paying them or hiring them full-time also".

Vedha let out a low whistle. "You thought this through"

"Of course, I did", she smiled even though he couldn't see it. "I just don't want you to give up on something you love because of practical obstacles. There's always a way"

"I will do it, Saira. This is such a cool idea". His voice was softer now, carrying something unspoken beneath it.

"Your words don't carry everything your heart wants to, do you like this idea?" asked Saira.

"Saira, yes. This is a great idea, I was just upset with you saying, there's always a way for everything but not us", rambled Vedha.

Saira exhaled loudly, expressing her loss of hope for life that played a fate game. She froze for a moment, his words settling into her like an unexpected wave.

His voice was steady and challenging. "You just told me there's always a way. So, why can't you apply that to yourself? You better know what that way is for you, isn't it, Saira?"

"Hmm, I had a way", she stopped. "Had? What was that?" he asked.

"If at all, I married someone I get the freedom, provided he is a gentle man who thinks he is none to give me my freedom", smirked Saira.

"Now?" Vedha asked with a little shock.

"I don't think I would ever marry anyone, even a gentleman", said she in a serious tone.

Vedha froze for a brief moment. The world around him dulled, and all he could hear were those words echoing in slow motion in his mind.

"I don't think I would ever marry anyone, even a gentleman".

His heart weighed heavily as he understood exactly what she meant, and that realisation twisted something deep inside him because she wasn't saying that she did not believe in marriage. She wasn't saying that she wanted to stay single by choice. She meant to say that she had no choice at all, and the one behind this decision of hers should have to be 'him'.

Vedha looked away suddenly, he felt like a thief pointing indirectly at him. A thief who had not just stolen her heart, but her hope. Her hope of getting a gentleman who can support her in her passion. But he never meant to. He never wanted to be the reason that she felt trapped in an impossible love. He swallowed hard, forcing himself to speak, but his voice felt distant. "Saira, don't say that"

While Saira was already crying, she still smiled softly, but it wasn't a happy smile. "It's just the truth", she uttered.

And that again made it worse. She wasn't blaming him. She wasn't demanding anything now. She had simply accepted her fate, the one he had unknowingly written into her life.

Vedha clenched his jaw. He wished he could fix this, but how can he fix something that should never have broken in the first place?

He let out a slow breath, gripping the phone tighter. "Saira…" he started. The words stuck in this throat. What could he even say? That he was sorry? That she deserve better? That she should move on? None of it would change the fact that she had made this decision because of him.

Saira remained quiet because she wasn't waiting for any reassurance. She wasn't hoping for a different answer. She had already made peace with it. And that was exactly what made Vedha feel worse.

"You don't have to do this to yourself." His voice was low, hesitant, almost pleading. "Life is unpredictable, Saira. You don't know what's waiting for you ahead."

She let out a small laugh, empty, hollow. "Yeah, I don't. But I know what's not waiting for me."

Both of them were crying at their ends, without deliberately showing each other. There existed a brief moment of silence again.

"I shouldn't have entered your life", the guilt clawed his chest.

"No, I wasn't meaning that. It wasn't your fault either", Saira compromised him. Vedha closed his eyes. He hated how much that truth hurt.

"But you don't deserve this", his voice was laced with frustration at himself, at the situation, at the helplessness of it all. "You don't deserve to hold on to something that will never change. You should—"

"Forget you?" she finished for him, a sad smile playing on her lips. "If it were that easy, I would have done it a long time ago."

Vedha had no response to that.

Saira did not like the tone the conversation was taking. The melancholic nonsense. The heaviness and sadness lingering between them were suffocating again, and she had had enough of it. She wiped her tears with her nightshirt collar and forced herself to take a deep breath. With a sudden energy shift, she spoke up with a light but bright tone as if she could wrap all the sadness and throw it far away from their reach.

"Okay, chuck all these. Imagine…." she said, a teasing lilt creeping into her voice, "if at all you had married me, your life would have been so much easier".

Vedha blinked, momentarily caught off guard by the abrupt change in her tone. "Huh?"

"Yeah", she gave an assuring tone. "Think about it! You would have started your garage in the very early years of your career. I would have handled all the management stuff while you were busy with college."

She grinned on the phone, determined to push the conversation toward something lighter. "I'm the one behind this sheer brilliance idea now, so it's only fair that I run things too, right?"

Vedha couldn't help it. He laughed out loud. A real, genuine laugh that loosened some of the tension in his chest.

"Oh, so now you're claiming my entire business?" he teased, playing along. "Next, you'll say I should be paying you for the idea, too."

"Obviously", she gasped dramatically. "It's called intellectual property rights, Mr. Vedha. You owe me big time".

Vedha was thrilled as he uncovered a new version of Saira. She used to be calm and quiet and felt lost because she couldn't pursue her dreams and then pursue her love with Vedha, but this tone of hers and the cheer were different from what he fixed herself to be. Vedha shook his head, amused. "Unbelievable".

Her words and charm stirred deeper emotions in him. A fleeting image of a completely different life from now, where Saira was his wife, managing the shop with her sharp mind and boundless energy, waiting for him after college, teasing him about his business decisions, laughing over the late-night talks. A life where he could come home to her. It wasn't his reality, and it never would be. Yet, he did not stop her, he let her talk. He let her fill the space between them with "what could have been". He just wanted to live in the imagined world with her just a little longer.

Saira spoke with a kind of playful certainty as if she had already lived that life in another timeline, it came out so naturally that even Vedha could almost believe it. "Just imagine", she continued, her voice painting a picture that felt too vivid and too warm to be mere imagination.

"Our garage would be bustling with students learning under you, and I'll be handling all the chaos at the counter with my sleeves rolled on and arguing with suppliers over the phone with a clipboard in hand".

Vedha leaned back against the wall, closing his eyes and letting himself slip into the world she was weaving. And then after a long day, he would walk into the house filled with the aroma of whatever she had decided to experiment with in the kitchen. There would be late-night conversations on the balcony, tired laughter over cups of coffee and lazy Sunday mornings where she would refuse to let him work, dragging him to the market instead, insisting, "An engineer should know how to pick vegetables too", and a life which wasn't theirs. His heart ached at the warmth of a dream he could never have.

Saira continued, her voice filled with excitement. "I would have a home library that has all my favourite fiction and books. A cosy space at home filled with stories and emotions, and that would be my favourite space at our home. We would both be chasing our dreams, but at the end of the day, we would come home to the same place. The same small, peaceful home just the way we want it to be. Late-night talks on the terrace under the moonlight, watching street lights with our shared ideas, and arguing over whose day was harder"

Vedha chuckled with tears in his eyes, "You would claim your was harder".

"Obviously", she shot back playfully. "Managing an empire is no joke", she winked. They both laughed together, irrespective of the underlying ache beneath it.

Saira sighed. "If only life worked that way, huh?"

Vedha couldn't control his tears trembling in his eyes. Saira sensed his crying, too, and she was shedding some leftover tears, too.

"I want to see you now, Saira", he uttered, hardly.

"What? Now? It's already been 2 AM. Oops", she was shocked to see the time slip away like a snow frost that faced the sunlight.

"Yes, now. Right now", Vedha said firmly. "Over a video call?" queried Saira.

"Nah, can you come out of your room to the balcony?" Vedha said softly. "What? Are you kidding or feeling sleepy now?" mocked Saira.

"Come out, please", he said.

Saira frowned in confusion but got up anyway, pushing aside the curtains and opening the door. As she stepped down and stood on her balcony, cool air brushed against her skin, and she wrapped her arms around herself and looked around.

"Okay, I came out and what now?" she puzzled.

"Look down", his voice was barely above a whisper. "Near the main gate".

Saira's eyes widened as she spotted him standing at the entrance of her hostel campus, leaning against his bike behind the compound wall. His phone was still pressed to his ear, but his gaze was fixed on her, illuminated by the dim yellow glow of the streetlight. For a moment, she forgot to breathe. "What are you doing here?" she whispered, gripping the railing of her balcony.

"I wanted to say something, not just over the phone. In-person", he said with an unbreakable ray of vision towards her. Saira's heart beat faster. He bent down on his knees with the phone in one hand to his ear and, extending another hand, he said, "I love you, Saira".

Saira's throat tightened.

"I love you in a way that I can't undo", he added.

Saira wanted to run down the stairs to pull out the gap between them. She felt her whole world tilt, and her heart begged her to run down those stairs to crash into him and say her heart out, that she had buried inside her for so long.

She held the grill bars tight and leaned against the railing, "I have these bars. The ones keeping me from running down to you right now", she reminded him of the reality of not just the hostel, but also her fate that denied her from uniting with him.

He took a deep breath, trying to inculcate the actual meaning behind what she said. "Even if I leave, even if there's no future for us, I still need you to know. If everything in this damn world won't let me be with you, at least let me say it. At least let me love you in words, if nowhere else. At this moment, he remained on his knees.

"Come on, it's time to rise to your feet", Saira hurried.

Vedha let out a soft chuckle, shaking his head as he looked up at her, "You really know how to break a moment, don't you?"

Saira smirked, wiping the corner of her eye discreetly before crossing her arms again. "Come on, someone has to stop you from confessing like a tragic hero, which isn't helping either of us. So, better to get up and leave before we both end up in trouble".

Vedha sighed, running a hand through his hair before glancing around to make it casual. "I hope there aren't CCTV cameras watching this over. Otherwise, I would get banned from entering the campus forever, even before I could leave the job".

Saira let out a laugh, "Now that would be a shame", she teased. "Who is going to show up in the middle of the night for a dramatic love confession then?"

Vedha grinned, moving towards his bike and slightly leaning on the seat with his leg support. "Oh, so you admit that you like it?"

Saira rolled her eyes, but her smile betrayed her. "I love you too, Vedha".

Vedha couldn't resist the surge of excitement that shot through him. She said, and she called him Vedha. Since they started to talk, he had been insisting on her, dropping such formalities and just addressing him by his name, the way he wanted to hear from her, in her voice. And she finally did. A broad smile stretched across his face, and his heart drummed with a strange mix of triumph and doubt. He slanted his head back and laughed, "Saira, you have no idea what you have just done".

Upon the balcony, Saira frowned and was confused, "Is it?"

Vedha smirked and leaned forward on his bike, "You finally called me Vedha".

She blinked, replaying her own words in her mind, and then the realisation hit. Her cheeks flushed slightly, refraining from words from her mouth. But he saw it from a distance. Vedha laughed again, raising a hand in mock surrender. "Fine, but so you understand that this is a win for me. You are never going back to calling me anything else from now on".

Saira let a small smile tug at her lips and reminded him, "For another 2 days, isn't it? Yep, I'm good".

It hit him about his resignation and the last couple of days that were left in his notice period. He remained silent.

"Now, can you please go home?" Saira said gleefully.

"Do I have to?" he asked aloud to Saira but to himself, referring to his resignation. "You must have to", she answered. Maybe for both.

"Saira..." he dragged.

"A good husband listens to his wife" Saira adjusted her shirt collar. Vedha's lips let a small curve escape. "Okie wifey, good night". "Good night", Saira said, blushing.

He revved his engine and finally rode off with a heart a little lighter than before. And she stood there watching him disappear into the night. It was 3 PM, and she locked the room and lay on the bed, replaying all that had happened. They lived in their talks, and it felt like they lived years together. The same thoughts cradled her into sleep.

# DAY 6: Night of wild thrills

The next morning, Saira slept through her alarm and woke up with a start at 7.30 in the morning. The moment her eyes shot open, she realised that she had missed her college bus. In the last two and a half years, she has never taken even a sick leave and has never missed the bus.

"Damn it", she groaned throwing off her blanket and scrambling out of bed.

Her head was still a little hazy from the late-night conversations with Vedha and his cute, dramatic 3 AM proposal. She couldn't ignore a smile, but she pressed her finger against her eyes, rubbing and trying to wake up. She quickly grabbed her phone and dialled Anya's number. After a couple of rings, Anya picked up. "Hey, what's up, Saira? Should I have to come to the cafeteria, the love birds have a new story?" she mocked Saira.

"Save the sarcasm, please, I missed my bus", sighed Saira. "Oh oh oh..." dragged Anya sarcastically.

"Come on, Anya. It's already late. Where are you?"

Anya chuckled, "Relax, I'm still about 10 minutes away from your hostel. I'll pick you up". "You are a lifesaver, Anya! I owe you one."

"You owe me at least ten by now, but who's counting?" Anya teased. "Now you get ready, or I'm leaving you behind"

Saira grinned, already hurrying to get dressed. "I'll be down in five".

As she rushed to freshen up and throw on her clothes, she couldn't help but steal a glance at her phone, half expecting a text from Vedha. There was nothing. She was not intentional anymore, but it's become a habit for her to check her phone for him.

She brushed and took a quick 1-minute shower, pulled her comfort clothes from her wardrobe and rushed to wear them. She took her bag and one last look in the mirror and ran downstairs. Anya was already there near her gate. Saira walked fast towards her and sat on her bike. And they moved.

"Hmm..Hmm…why did my sleeping beauty miss her bus today?" Anya teased as Saira gripped Anya's shoulders. The front mirror showed Anya how Saira rolled her eyes with a simple smile. "Don't start, Anya. Just drive".

Anya smirked, stealing a glance at her, "It was him, wasn't it?" "Huh?!" Saira's eyes widened in shock.

Anya wiggled her eyebrows. "I mean, was it him over the phone I asked?" grinning mischievously with her tone dripping with a playful suspicion."

Saira let out a breath she hadn't realised she was holding.

Anya laughed, enjoying his. "Oho, look at you panicking. I was just talking about the call. But now..." she leaned in slightly with her eyes twinkling, "I surely smell something more..."

Saira groaned as if she didn't believe a word. "There is nothing, I just overslept, okay?" Then Anya hummed as if she did not believe a word. "Hmm, overslept because of him?"

Saira shot a glare. "Anya, do you want to drop me at college or in the middle of the road?"

Anya burst into laughter, shaking her head. And they heard a sharp "beep beep" that interrupted their conversation.

Saira instinctively turned back, and Anya adjusted her rearview mirror. It was Vedha with his helmet on, bike revving slightly, with his gaze fixed on Saira.

"Hmmm hmmm", Anya cleared her throat while Saira let out a blushed smile. "Beep-beep-beep", he came parallel to them by their side.

"Hah! Beep-beep. Oh, please, that's too late now. I already cleared the road for him long ago", Anya said.

Saira's eyes blushed, catching the double meaning instantly. "Anya!" she exclaimed, shooting her glare.

"I just told the truth, dude", smirked Anya. "You are impossible", chuckled Saira.

"Ok, now you might get down in the middle of the road, too. There is someone ready on board to pick you up", Anya mocked again.

Saira huffed, still blushing, enjoying the moment. They reached the college in the next three minutes, and Vedha diverted to his bike stand while Anya and Saira continued till they reached the students' parking lot on the college grounds, and they walked straight to their classroom as it had already been the start time of their lectures.

They rushed to their class and froze for a moment to see the professor already in. It was their first time arriving late, and the college professors did not question the studious ones; there was still a moment of tension as they hesitated at the doorway. The professor glanced at them over the rim of his glasses with his sharp gaze, but not unkind. After a pause, he simply nodded toward their empty seats.

"Take your places".

Saira and Anya were relieved, and they quickly slipped into their respective spots, trying to blend in as if they had been there the whole time. Saira pulled out her notebook, pretending to be fully sunk in the lecture already, while Anya leaned in slightly and whispered, "That was close."

Saira sighed, shaking her head. "Yep, too close."

But even as she tried to focus, her mind kept drifting back to that 'beep-beep'. But, somehow, for some time, it kept her awake. She could hardly manage to stay awake for even half an hour. The late-night conversations and the monotonous drone of the professor's voice coupled together hit her like a wave of exhaustion. Her eyelids grew heavier with every passing minute until eventually, they shut down involuntarily.

"Unbelievable", Anya muttered under her breath. She nudged Saira's arms with her elbow, whispering, "Aye, sleeping beauty, wake up if you don't want to be called out by him".

Saira stirred, blinking drowsily, "Huh, yeah yeah… I'm listening", she mumbled through her voice that barely carried any conviction.

"Hmm...Hmm, totally doomed. Vedha-doomed", Anya grinned.

And that woke up Saira. She shot Anya a glare, but Anya just winked before returning to her notes. Saira sighed. She had no escape from anything at that moment. Neither her sleeplessness nor Anya's teasing nor her lingering thoughts about that 'beep-beep'.

Somehow, Saira battled the drowsiness creeping over her with Anya's generous stash of candies. Every time she felt her droop, Anya would slide a toffee or mint toward her with a smirk, "Here, stay alive."

Saira unwrapped one sluggishly, popping it into her mouth, hoping the high sugar levels would keep her from slipping back into sleep. It helped a little. Anya, enjoying Saira's struggle far too much, leaned in and whispered, "You better get used to it, or should I carry extra coffee shots for you now?"

Saira shot her a tired glance, "Just let me die in peace"

Anya chuckled," Oh no, you are not dying. You are just sleep-deprived. Courtesy of a certain someone who goes beep-beep?"

Saira groaned, resting her forehead on the desk, "I hate you".

"Liar", Anya grinned, passing another candy. "Come on! Stay up, don't drool".

Saira sighed, unwrapping it in defeat. This was going to be a long lecture.

And then finally, the bell rang for the lunch break. The moment Saira had been desperately waiting for. She wasted no time and rushed to the washroom to eagerly shake off the last remnants of sleep. Leaning over the wash basin, she splashed cold water onto her face, letting it drip down her skin, washing away all the grogginess.

Anya stood beside her, casually fixing her hair. Looking at the mirror image of her, she teased, "Feeling alive now?"

Saira exhaled, grabbing a tissue and dabbing it. She said, "Barely, at least I won't collapse".

"Good, because I can't drag your unconscious body to the cafeteria. Now let's go before all the good food is gone".

Saira nodded with a slightly more awake feeling. They both walked toward the cafeteria and sat in their usual places, singing with their plates.

"Hmm, but you are not escaping this conversation, Miss Mysterious!" declared Anya, blocking Saira's way with a mischievous grin.

"What conversation?" Saira asked with feigning innocence. "The late-night Vedha Sir lectures", Anya winked.

"Fine", Saira sighed, taking a bite of her food. "We talked about his passion last night. I suggested a way for him to make it work. Like, he could include his students in his garage to work for experience without worrying about paying salaries and do it outside of college hours, so he has continuous earnings while also following his dream. Initially, it would seem like hard work, and it perpetually is, but no dreams are ever easier to achieve anyway, aren't they?"

Anya justed out her lower lip in a playful mock, but also intrigued. She leaned forward, "Oh? And what did Sir Beep-Beep say?"

Saira twirling her spoon in her rice absentmindedly, "He liked the idea and said it was feasible".

Aya nodded, "Makes sense. And then?"

"And then he turned the question on me", she admitted with a softer voice. "He said likewise, I have also got some other way to pursue my dream and asked, why can't I do something about my passion?"

Anya's expression shifted from teasing to something more thoughtful. "Hmm, and what did you say?"

Saira exhaled deeply to release the heaviness of unspoken thoughts. "What else, Anya? Don't you know my dad?" Her voice carried both frustration and resignation. "I have already asked him a few times ... even the very last month when I went to my home. And I simply end up discouraging hearing his piece of advice. She traced invisible patterns on the table with her fingers, lost in thought, "But, what can I even say to Vedha now? It's not like I can openly complain to him about it. Instead, I just spoke generally about how a woman always needs permission to pursue their passion and how we constantly seek approval for the things we dream of."

"Hmm, to dream is not a woman's birthright most of the time", Anya said to herself.

Saira let out a dry laugh, shaking her head. "I rambled about all that, thinking he would get the hint and drop it. But no. He kept pressing and kept asking what my passion was. And then, somehow, the topic got diverted, and I never really answered him". Her voice trailed off as she stared at nothing in particular, lost in the thoughts of how complicated it was for her to even think of going behind her dreams"

"Hmm…" dragged Anya so that she couldn't deny what Saira said. She took another spoonful of rice from her plate when Saira almost hesitantly added, "And…he kind of proposed to me at 2 AM".

Anya choked. "What?" she coughed, setting her spoon down before she could spill it over herself? Saira sighed. She was expecting this exact reaction from Anya. "Lower your voice, Anya!" she hissed, glancing around to make sure no one was eavesdropping.

Anya was still in shock and leaned in closer. "Excuse me?! Back up! Vedha sir? I mean..married Vedha sir proposed to you at 2 AM??! What in the dramatic cinema script is happening here?!"

Saira rubbed her forehead, regretting bringing it up, but there was no turning back now. "It wasn't like that, Anya. Whether he is saying it or not, we know it already, right? He said, "Even if nothing can change, he needs me to know and hear the same from him".

"Okay, this makes sense as well", Anya let out a gasp. "So, basically, he managed to mess with both your heart and your morning routine. Impressive."

"Hmm…not with my heart this time, it's only the other one", Saira assured. "Sure?" asked Anya.

Saira nodded. They finished their lunches, and as they reached their class, they found the class empty. And then they realised it was a laboratory hour and rushed to the lab with their record notes and lab coats. Somehow, the lab session was over, and as usual, Saira sat by the window. The bus was filling up with students, and the usual chatter and laughter were echoing around her. But she was elsewhere anticipating. And then there he was. Vedha walked past with his usual confident, unshaken stride, his gaze, the one she had grown so used to, felt lighter than it used to. It was merely a continuation of their conversation, an unspoken, "I meant every word I said".

"I knew", she gazed back, averting her eyes in time to check if anyone was catching them up. And then as the bus moved, Saira reached her hostel in another 20 minutes. She had never been the one to call him first; it was always Vedha who reached out and broke the silence. It was he, all five days, who found a reason to keep their conversations. But, today, Saira craved to call him and talk to him without wasting a single minute because she realised it was the day before his final day in college. Tomorrow being the last working day upon his resignation, her heart pounded heavily at to imagine that she was not seeing him anymore. Even if he is within her reach, she wouldn't do what she promised herself not to do.

She sat on her bed, gripping her phone tightly. Taking a deep breath, she pressed the call option before she could overthink calling him first. The dial tone rang. Once, twice and thrice. Her pulse quickened with each second that passed. And then, click. "Hello", his voice was heard.

Saira exhaled, not realising she had been holding her breath. "Hi, hope I'm not disturbing you," she said.

"Not at all, this is a historic moment, and I just thought I should mark the date. You called me, Saira?" he uttered with warmth.

There was a pause, and Saira's unusual silence was smelled by Vedha. "Oi", what happened? Are you fine?" he was concerned.

"I was quite fine until I remembered tomorrow is your last working day", her voice laced with an emotion she couldn't quite mask.

"Uff", he exhaled for a moment, and there was only silence. "I have already completed all my formalities, and I just have to leave tomorrow like any other day. So, I least realised it. But, now as you say, I can realise how six days flew by like a breeze, Saira."

Saira leaned back against the cold wall, staring at the ceiling.

As a student interrupted him, he hung up, conveying the same to Saira. She was accommodating her thoughts between the moments she enjoyed with him and the moments that had never been written for her anymore. She waited for another half an hour, sunk in this melancholy, until he called back and said, "Saira, can we make this evening special?" he asked.

"What's so special about us being hit by our realities?" lamented Saira.

"Come on, Saira. We knew our fate. It's not today we discover it, right?" he said.

He reminded her of the intention she had when she started to talk to him. But, it was heavily to accept this, especially on the verge of ending.

"So, what can we do?" she asked him.

"I don't want the night to end like this", he said. "Come out with me, one last time, please?". Her breath hitched. "Now?"

"Yes, the night. Entire night. Just you and me".

She glanced at the door of her room, then at the barred window on the first floor of the hostel. Her mind screamed impossible, but something deeper, something reckless inside her whispered to her to break the rule because it was the last night.

She shut her eyes, her mind racing. Every logical part of her told her to stay in her room, to let him go, to accept what was inevitable. But another part, the one that had long been caged by expectations, rules and fears, was desperate to breathe.

"But, how do I get out of my hostel? I cannot lie to the warden or even say that I will be back to my room after some time, my dad has an informer here", she shivered.

"Make it somehow, Saira. Tell me you are going to your friend's house. We will come back to the room after 5 in the morning", there was silence, and "Not possible?" asked him.

"No, not like that, can you give me 5 minutes?" asked her. "Yep, call me back", he hung up.

Saira called Anya. It rang. Anya picked.

"Hmm…hmm, what's up, madam? Mr. Vedha Sagar hasn't started his lectures yet?" mocked Anya.

"Anya, come on. I need your help, and it's kind of urgent now", she said.

Anya raised her eyebrow, intrigued, "Oh, sounds serious. What kind of help? Are we plotting a rebellion?" she teased at first. As she felt the silence between them, she straightened up. "Okay, spill it. What's going on?"

Saira glanced around, making sure she talked about what she wanted to convey to her. She lowered her voice. "I need to get out tonight. Not through the front gate. Over the compound wall."

Anya's eyes first widened, and then they narrowed mischievously. "Wait, wait… You?" Anya was shocked.

"The same Saira who follows every rule like it's the law of the universe? You're telling me you want to sneak out of the hostel? And for what? Vedha sir?"

Saira bit her lip hesitating for seconds before she nodded and continued, "It's his last day here, Anya. I don't know why, but I feel like if I let this moment go, I'll regret it forever. I just… I just want to see him one last time without any barriers", she dragged, "help me please, I'm clueless", pleaded Saira.

"You realise there are CCTV cameras, right? You'd get caught before you even landed on the other side", scared Anya.

"Oh, please, don't fuel my fear, Anya, that was exactly why I called for an idea. Please help me with your mastermind", continued Saira.

Anya tapped her chin, thinking. "Hmm… If you're serious about this, we'll have to time it right. I might just have a way to create a distraction. But you, my dear Saira, better be ready to jump."

Saira's heart pounded. She didn't know if it was from excitement or fear, but for the first time in a long while, she felt alive.

Saira gave a pause. And said, "Okay, what to do, now?"

Saira listened carefully as Anya explained the plan, "Okay, so I'll come near the hostel and create a distraction for the watchman. Meanwhile, I'll also get updates from your hostel mates about the safest spot to jump from, one that's not covered by CCTV," Anya said confidently.

"How do they know the safest spot?"

"Saira, my innocent puppy, you are the one who lies like a bookworm in your hostel, most of them would have jumped from that safest spot a year before itself", mocked Anya.

"Oh", Saira dragged, assuring herself that she was not doing anything that sounded like a crime, or just something abnormal.

Saira bit her lip. "And what will you tell the watchman?"

Anya smirked. "Oh, don't worry about that. I can be very convincing. I'll make something up, maybe act like I'm here to meet someone, or say I lost my wallet nearby. You just focus on getting out".

Saira took a deep breath as the weight of what she was about to do sank in. She had never broken a rule like this before. But tonight wasn't about rules. It was about breaking free.

"Okay, done", exhaled Saira.

"I will start from here in another 5 minutes and will reach your hostel in a maximum of 20 minutes. Get ready", Anya hung up.

Anya was the free-spirited one, not the 'free-spirit' that girls write on their Instagram bio and still keep their accounts private, upon their parents' rules. The real free spirit who had no trouble leaving her house. Her parents weren't overly strict as long as she kept them informed about her whereabouts. She casually told them she was stepping out and hopping on her scooter, heading straight to Saira's hostel.

Meanwhile, Saira called Vedha.

"Hello," she rushed. "I will leave the hostel in another 15 minutes. But where should I come?"

He thought for a moment and said, "I will send the location to Saira. It's just 15 minutes from your hostel. We will meet there".

"Okay, sure. Send me soon", she hung up.

Vedha was excited to spend the night with his favourite girl. And he can't wait for the moment. He announced to his students that he would leave earlier today, almost by 8 PM.

Saira again dressed up for a date night. But it was the most thrilling night, probably in her entire lifetime. She picked her favourite yellow kurti, matched it to her blue chinos and carefully avoided wearing the shawl, but kept it folded in her handbag. She carefully folded the cash she saved and placed it securely in her handbag. It wasn't much, just the money her father gave her whenever she visited home, but tonight, it felt like a symbol of her little independence and her own choice.

She looked at her reflection in the mirror. The straight pants and kurti gave her a composed, mature look. It wasn't just about looking good now, it was about feeling ready. It almost felt like she was ready to break free from every limitation, every unspoken rule that had kept her caged.

On the way, Anya messaged Saira, "I'm almost there. Be ready. It's going to be legendary."

As she fastened her watch and picked up her phone, her heart pounded in excitement. 'This is happening.'

Just then, her phone vibrated. It was Anya.

"Saira, I'm just ten feet ahead of the main gate", she fastened. "The right corner of the gate is our best bet," Anya had informed her. "There's a tree sitting right there, and its shadow covers the CCTV camera's view. That's your way out."

Saira nodded, her heart racing with excitement and nervousness.

"You need to come out and take a right immediately," Anya continued. "And when you jump over the compound wall, make sure no one is behind you. The last thing you want is to be caught in the act."

Saira took a deep breath, gripping her handbag tightly as she listened carefully. "One more thing," Anya added, lowering her voice.

"There's a cycle stand right outside the wall. So, be careful when you land. Don't hit the cycles, or worse, knock them over. If that happens, you'll get spotted for sure."

Saira swallowed hard. This was it. She wasn't just sneaking out for a night with Vedha. She was breaking through the invisible walls she had always lived within. Her heart pounded, but she knew she had to do this.

"You come out, be placed on the spot, you are going to jump and then leave a message to me, I will start distracting the watchman", said Anya before she hung up the call.

Saira locked her room carefully, her fingers trembling slightly as she twisted the key. A quiet sigh escaped her lips. I should return safely, just as I am leaving, she wished silently. It felt like such an old-fashioned thought, something her mother or grandmother might say before stepping out.

But that was just how her mind worked at the time. Very cautious, structured, and always preparing for every possible outcome. Even in a moment of rebellion, a part of her still epigenetically craved security.

With one final glance at her room, she pressed her handbag against her chest, took a deep breath, and stepped forward, ready to break her boundaries.

She texted Anya that she had reached the spot. A message from Anya came in a minute.

"I'm here. Watchman is distracted. You know what to do. Be quick!"

Saira finally leapt, her heart pounding as she landed softly on the other side of the compound wall. The moment her feet touched the ground, a rush of exhilaration mixed with fear coursed through her veins. I did it, she thought, barely having a second to revel in her tiny victory before she heard voices from the other side.

Anya was still inside, keeping the plan intact, arguing with the watchman in a deliberately loud voice. But, she heard the dried leaves being stamped on her jump, indicating that the task was accomplished. But, still, Anya continued to give the raw essence to the adventurous play.

"I'm telling you, uncle! This is so unfair! How can you say no now? You let us stay out late during the festival night, didn't you?"

Saira smirked as she crouched behind the row of parked cycles outside, waiting for the right moment to move. Anya was playing her role perfectly, and Saira couldn't afford to get caught now.

She took a deep breath and, without turning back, she started walking briskly toward the main street where there were cabs and auto rickshaws.

After a while, Anya wrapped up her act, letting out a dramatic sigh as she ended the argument with the poor, confused watchman. "Fine, fine! I'll go. But just know, this is so unfair!" she huffed, stomping away to where her bike was parked.

She started the engine, the familiar roar cutting through the quiet night. Riding out of the hostel gate at a steady pace, she made sure not to seem rushed or suspicious.

Once she was a safe distance away, she pulled over near a dimly lit street corner and pulled out her phone.

She dialled Saira's number and put the call on speaker. "Alright, runaway bride, where are you?" she teased.

Saira exhaled in relief before answering, "Waiting for the cab, Anya. You?" "Right corner of where you are waiting".

Saira searched and waved at Anya as she found her. Anya waved back. "And Saira..." Anya revving her scooter.

"Yeah?"

"Tell Vedha he owes me one for this", Anya added playfully. "I will", Saira chuckled, though her heart was still racing.

The cab pulled up in front of her with its headlights briefly illuminating her nerves, yet she wore an excited face. She quickly opened the door and slid inside, exhaling as she gave the location Vedha had sent her.

As the car started moving, she rested her head back, her thoughts spinning. This was it, she thought and exhaled. She was breaking boundaries, literally and figuratively. There was no turning back now.

Her phone buzzed. It was Vedha. "Did you make it out?"

She smiled to herself and replied, "On my way".

Vedha was excited, but for Saira, this was a night of 'firsts', and it was beyond excitement just seeing Vedha.

It was the first time she had travelled alone in a metropolitan city, navigating unfamiliar roads without anyone's permission. The first time she booked a cab on her own, relying solely on herself. The first time she broke free from the invisible chains that had always held her back.

She looked out of the window as the city lights blurred past her. The streets were alive, yet she felt like she was in a world of her own, one where she was finally in control. Her heart raced, but not out of fear. It was out of an exhilarating realisation that she had decided this for herself.

It always hits at a different level when we finally take all the power back. When we stop waiting for permission and start prioritising ourselves, the decisions, the choices, the priorities, and the responsibilities, everything shifts into our own hands.

For Saira, this wasn't just about sneaking out of her hostel or meeting Vedha. It was about reclaiming herself. For the first time, she wasn't just a daughter following orders, a student abiding by rules, or a girl confined by expectations. She was Saira, the young woman who chose herself, who chose her life.

She felt the weight of years lifting off her shoulders, replaced by the lightness of freedom. She didn't know where this night would lead, but for now, she let herself revel in the fact that she had chosen it. She had chosen herself.

The phone buzzed again. Vedha asked, "Nervous?"

She hesitated before typing back. "More. But I'm also excited."

For the first time in her life, it wasn't a lie.

Saira reached into her bag and pulled out the neatly folded shawl, and with deliberate care, she draped it over her left shoulder. Once a simple piece of fabric that had accompanied her on mundane days, tonight it transformed into her quiet armour, like a reminder of the boundaries she was determined to break.

In that dark, solitary moment, with the urban landscape unfurling outside the window, Saira felt the weight of her past lifting. She knew that every step she took tonight was a declaration of independence. A choice made solely for her own sake. Sometimes, just 'falling in love' makes all the difference by pulling out the unknown, hidden versions of ourselves.

The venue was reached in 15 minutes. She chose to pay in cash, knowing that any other online method would leave a record neither with the place nor the person nor the exact time. She couldn't risk her father finding out.

Just as Saira reached for her wallet, ready to pay, she noticed a familiar figure standing near the cab.

"Professor Vedha Sagar".

Before she could even react, he stepped forward and leaned toward the driver's window. "How much?" he asked.

The driver told him the fare, and before Saira could protest, Vedha pulled out his phone, scanned the code and paid the charge.

Vedha, without a word, reached past her and shut the car door. She turned slightly to see him already pulling out his phone to pay.

"I had cash," she muttered, feeling a mix of gratitude and resistance.

"I know," he said, scanning the code and settling the fare. "But let me do this."

There was something about the way he said it. A kind of gentleness yet unwavering that silenced her from saying anything back. The driver nodded and drove away, leaving them standing under the dim streetlight. The city hummed in the background, but at that moment, all she could hear was the quiet excitement between them.

And they stood at the same place exchanging a powerful, unyielding glance that spoke volumes without a single word out of their mouths. The silent exchange was as if both of them acknowledged that they had finally arrived, like the countless barriers, the late-night confessions, and all the unspoken promises converged in that one charged moment. For Saira, it was more than just a physical escape; also the culmination of her inner rebellion, a declaration of her newfound independence. And for Vedha, it was the bittersweet recognition that this night, this fleeting moment of freedom, felt like a testament to everything they had dared beyond their hesitations and norms. In each other's eyes, they found the unspoken message, "We are finally here".

Vedha looked at her, "Thank you, Saira", his voice softer than usual. "For coming beyond your comfort zone, for doing this for us..."

Saira smiled, shaking her head, "Probably, I should be the one more thankful to you. I realised how much I was daring to stand up for myself, I never thought I had this in me".

Vedha crossed his arms. "Great, can we debate who is more thankful to whom?"

Saira chuckled, "My gut is staging a protest, feed me before I fade, please" She nudged him playfully, "I broke the rule, I jumped walls, and I sneaked out. Breaking rules burns calories", she waved her hands in pride.

Vedha laughed at her gesture. He reached for his bike helmet and handed her one. "Hop on, madam. Let's find you the best midnight feast of your life"

Saira climbed onto the bike behind him, adjusting her shawl. Vedha turned slightly, glancing over his shoulder. With a small tilt of his head, he signalled her to hold on. Saira hesitated for a second, then slowly placed her hands on his shoulders. Even through the fabric of his jacket, she could feel the warmth of his body. It was different, closer and more real than ever before.

"Comfortable?" he asked, his voice teasing but gentle.

She nodded, though he couldn't see her. "Just drive", she murmured, tightening her grip ever so slightly. With a smirk, he revved the engine, and they sped off into the night, the wind carrying their unspoken feelings between them.

Every delicate wisp of air she drew in carried a storm within what she never thought she'd experience. The night, she first scrolled through Facebook and saw his wedding photos, the moment her heart clenched with a pain she couldn't name, the day she confronted him to admit that she wasn't the only one feeling this strange, unspoken connection, the evening when he finally opened his heart, and she realized how deeply tangled they had become, none of it prepared her for this.

She never imagined that fate, despite its cruelty, would allow her this moment. Riding on his bike, holding onto him, feeling the rhythm of his breath and the warmth of his presence, all those felt unreal to her. It felt like something out of a dream, a stolen piece of happiness she wasn't sure she was allowed to have.

But for now, she let herself have it.

As they arrived at the restaurant, Saira stepped down from the bike, adjusted her shawl, and took a moment to breathe in the night air. And Vedha manoeuvred his bike into the parking space. Saira admired his effortless and familiar movements as if he had done this a hundred times before, the way he carefully turned the handlebars and positioned the bike, the way he moved with ease and even the smallest gestures. From a distance, she watched as he removed his helmet and ran a hand through his slightly tousled hair, shaking off the remnants of the wind. Simple act, but so natural and unguarded. She had had opportunities of just glancing at his walk, but never these gestures with this proximity, like the fleeting admiration turned out to be real, present and unfolding right in front of her.

Just then, Vedha turned, catching her in the middle of her thoughts. His lips curled into a subtle smirk, his eyes filled with amusement. "What?" he asked, his voice teasing yet soft.

"Nothing", she hid, but her smile betrayed her.

Vedha chuckled, shaking his head as he walked toward her. "Come on, let's eat. I'm starving too." She followed him inside, unable to hide the small, secret smile forming on her lips.

They had no room for doubt. No more formalities between them. They ate like they had done this many times before, as if sharing meals had always been their thing. Unlike the first time, which was just a day before, where every movement was careful, every glance filled with the weight of unsaid words, tonight felt undemanding.

Saira didn't mind when Vedha took a bite out of her dish without asking. She followed suit, using her fingers to pick up a bit of his food and taste it as if it were instinctive. Somewhere between the shared nibbles and playful teasing, the walls that had separated them had silently collapsed, and their conversations blended in perfectly with the clinking of cutlery.

Vedha paid the bill, sliding his card across the counter before Saira could even think of reaching for her wallet. "It's all mine tonight," he said casually, stuffing the receipt into his pocket.

Saira rolled her eyes but didn't argue. There was something about the way he said it. Calm, certain, like it wasn't even up for discussion.

As they stepped outside, Vedha walked ahead, heading toward his bike, while Saira lingered a few steps behind, watching him. His every movement was familiar now, yet still fascinating. The way he adjusted his sleeves, the way he ran a hand through his hair before putting on his helmet, the way his presence itself felt like something solid, grounding her in a way she hadn't even realised she needed.

He swung a leg over his bike and settled in place before glancing at her. "So, where to next?"

She crossed her arms, feigning deep thought. "I wish I could honestly answer you," she admitted, "but I won't."

They exchanged unwavering glances with smiles.

"Where do you want to take me?" he whispered him fiddling with his tongue. "A mall", she said.

"Mall?" Vedha was amazed.

"Yes, yes, before its 10 o'clock, before the doors were sealed for the day, please", Saira asked him.

Vedha let out a soft chuckle, shaking his head before gunning the engine. Without another word, he sped off and surged his bike forward with an energy that matched the electricity between them.

They reached the mall in no time. Vedha smoothly parked his bike in the lot. As Saira hopped down, she adjusted her shawl and, without hesitation, walked alongside him toward the entrance. She appeared confident, like she had already been to that place, but this was her first time stepping into a mall since she moved to the city. As they passed through the glass doors, the cool air-conditioned breeze hit her face, making her suddenly aware of how surreal this night was turning out to be. She was out with him on a night she sneaked out of her hostel. With absolutely no permission or excuse. And now, here she was, walking beside him like it was the most natural thing to do.

"Where to?" Vedha asked casually. Saira turned to one of the shop assistants standing nearby. "Men's section?" she inquired politely. The shop helper smiled and gestured toward the escalator. "Second floor, ma'am."

"Thank you," Saira replied and turned to Vedha and without giving him a chance to ask why, she started walking toward the escalator, leaving him slightly puzzled but willingly following her.

As they stepped onto the moving stairs, Saira clutched the railing. She tried not to let the overwhelming feeling of being in a mall for the first time. But Vedha noticed the way her eyes darted around, taking in the glimmering lights, branded store names, and bustling crowds.

"First time here?" he asked gently, reading her.

Saira smiled faintly, embarrassed to admit it. "Kind of…"

Vedha didn't push further. Instead, he walked beside her as they reached the second floor with curiosity to know why she had asked for the men's section. Saira walked ahead with her eyes scanning through the neatly stacked displays of shorts and pants under different brand names. The warm overhead lights brightened every colour from the solid pastels to dark hues, from checked patterns to the plain ones. Her fingers brushed against the fabrics that fell into her liking categories as she walked along while carefully searching through the sections.

Vedha followed her, now highly suspicious about her intentions. "Casuals, ma'am?" she asked the staff, who then directed her to the right section. As she continued her search, Vedha slowly began to put the pieces together. A faint knowing smile crept onto his face. "Wait a second," he said, leaning toward her, "Am I the one who's going to get a purchase tonight?"

Saira turned slightly, caught off guard, but managed to play it cool. "Hmm… I never said that," she smirked, pretending to still look at the clothes. Vedha chuckled, shoving his hands into his pockets. "But you didn't deny it either," he teased, now deliberately slowing down his pace, letting her lead the hunt.

Saira couldn't help but smile to herself as she walked toward a shelf with a row of perfectly folded casual shirts. She picked one in an earthy brown tee, held it against him from a little distance, and measured it visually. "This one suits you," she said.

Vedha raised a brow, stepping closer. "Really? Or are you just trying to find an excuse to spend money on me tonight?" Saira shook her head, trying to hold back her grin. "Well, it's not every day I take a man out on a shopping spree. So let me, please".

Vedha let out a deep laugh. "You're something, Saira."

"And you're lucky," she added slyly, pulling out another shirt in a light blue shade and placing it against his chest. "This one too", they exchanged a close breath with each other, "It'll match your vibe."

"My vibe?" he asked, intrigued.

"Hmm… simple, calm, and…" she trailed off, trying to find the right word.

"And what?" Vedha pressed.

Saira met his eyes briefly, "…and my favourite," she admitted in a low tone and then looked away, feeling the rush of heat crawling to her cheeks. Vedha froze for a moment, hearing those words that sounded much deeper than just a compliment. Before he could say anything, Saira swiftly turned to the staff. "Pack these two, please", she added fast, "Along with those blue chinos"

As she moved to the billing counter, he stopped her. "Saira, why?"

"Please", her eyes shrank in a way that reminded him she would soon leave her reality, but her favourite dress could still hold the imprints. He allowed himself to sink into her choices for him and stared at her for a second. As Saira walked toward the billing counter, casually chatting with the staff and carefully pulling out the small bundle of money with different denominations that clearly showed how much she would have saved from her pocket money, Vedha was still a few steps behind, watching her in silence.

Vedha never imagined someone, especially Saira, would do something like this for her. His gaze softened with an unbearable longing for how effortlessly she fit into his world tonight, crossing all her boundaries merely to spend a night with him. She stood there with confidence he had never seen in her before, handing over the money without a second thought, like it was always her thing to do.

He watched her delicate fingers clutching the paper bag, and her face lit up with satisfaction as she turned around searching for him. The moment her gaze met, he was overwhelmed and let 'falling deeper every second' kind of smile. As she came near him, she stood and carefully pulled the brown tee and the blue chinos from the paper bag with her eye scanning for the texture before nodding in satisfaction. She casually extended the outfit to Vedha.

He blinked, "Uh?"

She suppressed a laugh and said, "Trail room is right there" She pointed toward the rooms.

"Go", she nudged, "Look at you, tucked in a neatly ironed shirt. Too sophisticated and too rigid for me to vibe tonight. I want to see how casual you can look" A desperate look flickered in her narrow eyes. Vedha shook his head, amused, but he couldn't resist the sparkle in her eyes. He walked towards the trial room while Saira stood back smiling.

A few minutes later, the trial room door creaked open. Saira, who was already tapping her feet impatiently, paused and lifted her gaze. And there Vedha was. He stepped out, now clad in the casual brown t-shirt and blue chinos she picked for him. The rigidness of his personality seemed to melt away with those formalities he left behind. His hair was slightly ruffled, the casual fit effortlessly outlining his physique, and his aura felt lighter. Freer. More like a man and less like a professor.

Saira froze. She didn't expect this. Her lips parted slightly as she stared, unblinking, "God, this is dangerous".

Vedha caught her dazed expression and instinctively shot her a questioning look. "What?"

She snapped out of it. "Uh… nothing," she mumbled, but her lingering gaze on him betrayed her words.

His eyes didn't leave hers either, and for a brief moment, their unsaid thoughts collided like wild fireworks in silence. There was something very different about tonight, and they both knew it.

Vedha broke the trance, clearing his throat and walked toward her carrying his neatly folded formals in one hand. He gently grabbed the bag from her and slid his folded shirt and pants from inside. It wasn't the act itself. It was the way he did, that stirred Saira's heart, as if they had always belonged to each other's space. His touch grazed her fingers momentarily when he grabbed the bag, and she felt the rush of electricity sweep through her veins.

"Better?" he asked softly, referring to his new look, but his gaze stayed glued to hers like secretly asking something deeper. "Way better", she tried to sound casual.

He smiled, "Where next?"

She blinked, clueless, thrusting her lower lip.

"Well, now it's my choice", he said with a mischievous grin, slipping his hands into his new chinos' pockets.

"Where?" she asked curiously.

"That's for me to know and for you to find out, "he smirked, walking toward the elevator.

She followed him as he pressed the lift button. The lift was up, and as it opened, Vedha gestured, "After you". She smiled nervously, stepping inside, and he joined her.

As the doors of the lift shut, the silence between them thickened. For the first time, they were caught in the reflection of the elevator mirror, standing together like a couple, unintentionally perfect. Saira's breath hitched as she glanced at their reflection, her in a simple kurti and shawl, and him in the casuals she picked just a while ago. It felt like the universe suddenly played a cruel game of showing her how they could have looked together if life weren't as complicated.

Vedha, too, caught the reflection. His smirk faded slightly, his eyes now soaking in the sight of them side by side, like it was meant to be. "What are we doing here, Saira?" his mind whispered, but his heart refused to answer.

"You look good in casuals," Saira broke the silence. Her words were steady, but her voice held a shy undercurrent. Vedha turned toward her with a crooked smile. "And you look….like you belong next to me," he said in a tone too soft, yet too powerful to ignore.

Her stomach somersaulted, "Did he mean it?"

The lift opened with a ding. They broke their gaze hurriedly.

She stood outside the mall, clutching the paper bag with her heart still fluttering from the elevator moment. She spotted Vedha driving his bike from the parking lot toward her. His casual brown tee and blue chinos looked so effortless on him now, like he'd always belonged in them, and somehow she liked how she had a part in it tonight. He stopped the bike in front of her with a subtle chin lift and a silent, "Hop on".

She slung the paper bag over her shoulder and swiftly hopped onto the bike; her hands found his shoulders instinctively, like a muscle memory was already being built between them. And he drove off. She didn't ask where they were going, she didn't want to. Wherever Vedha took her tonight, she knew she would love it, simply because it was with him.

As minutes passed, she leaned slightly toward his back, feeling the warmth of his body as the night air turned colder. Her grip on his shoulders softened but stayed firm. For the first time, she wasn't afraid of holding onto what she desired. Vedha also did not want to reach their destination, as having her behind him like this and feeling her presence closely made him wish the night would never end.

As the bike sped up through the quiet night streets, the comfort of the ride and the warmth radiating from Vedha's back made Saira slowly drift off. Vedha felt the shift. Her fingers no longer clutched his shoulders but fell limply against his sides. A gentle smile crept up his face as he realised she had dozed off. Carefully, without startling her, he shifted his left hand from the handlebar, and gently tugged at the paper bag she was still clutching and gently slid it away from her grip. He placed the paper bag in front of him, resting it over the engine, ensuring it wouldn't fall off during the ride. With his left hand, he adjusted her hand to rest more comfortably on his waist.

A strange warmth flooded his chest. "Was it protectiveness? Was it the fact that she felt safe enough to sleep behind him? Or was it simply the bittersweet realisation that this moment, like everything else between them, was temporary?"

"Seriously, Saira, you chose now to sleep off?" he chuckled under his breath.

Her head slightly shifted in response, but she didn't wake up. A part of him selfishly didn't want her to. Because having her curled up behind him and trusting him like this felt like the purest form of closeness they'd shared so far. Because a woman feeling safe in a man's embrace is the deepest, most intoxicating form of grace. Real men are not moved by beauty, not the curves, not the sway of stance, but the quiet surrender of her trust in his hands.

He rode slower now, merely prolonging the journey, as if delaying their arrival would somehow make this night longer. He stole glances through the rearview mirror, watching her peaceful face, her hair tousled slightly from the wind. The air became salty and thick with the ocean's aroma as the bike began to slow down. Saira stirred from her slumber, slowly blinking awake as the cool, briny breeze caressed her face. The rhythmic crashing of the waves mingled with distant voices and loud music, indicating they had arrived at a vibrant place, even at this late hour.

Vedha carefully parked the bike, feeling the lingering weight of her sleepiness on his back. She lifted her head gradually and surveyed her surroundings, her drowsy eyes widening in wonder. The stretch of beach he had chosen to bring her to be still alive with activity. Colourful string lights hung heavily from every angle, brightening the shoreline. Groups of people lounged on the sand, some laughing, others engaged in profound conversations, while others danced joyfully in the open terrace restaurants, which sparkled like a beacon.

"You brought me here?" she asked, her voice still carrying the warmth of sleep.

Vedha turned back with a sly smile, "I told you, my choice now. I wanted you to see the city's heart even at night. It never sleeps, Saira. Just like us tonight."

She laughed softly, rubbing her eyes. The air was dense with freedom and the night's unspoken adventure. As she hopped off the bike, she noticed the sand beneath her sandals and the vast open darkness ahead, only interrupted by the shimmering moonlight on the sea. They both walked through the sand that was outside the fence that separated the deeper beach shore area. They entered an open terrace cafe that sat luxuriously overlooking the beach. The cafe radiated elegance with bright golden lights and glass walls with a polished wooden deck that extended into the open sky. The gentle sea breeze carried the aroma of roasted coffee beans, blending with the salty air, making the place heavenly in the late-night hour.

Vedha led her through the small stairway up to the terrace. Saira looked around in awe, the vast ocean with the orchestrating waves like the symphony of nature in the dark. It felt surreal to her. As she stood by there, Vedha reached the reception counter, as the receptionist greeted her, he nodded with a smile and "One cappuccino, please…and" he paused, holding the paper bag of his previous formals and a new blue shirt. "Can you please keep this bag safe here? I'll collect it later". The receptionist smiled warmly and nodded, "Sure, sir"

Handing over the bag to the receptionist, Vedha walked and stood behind Saira, who was still lost in the serenity of the ocean.

"Beautiful, isn't it?" he whispered in her ears so close, sending a warm rush down her spine. A pause.

Saira's heart drummed fiercely inside her chest as she felt his breath lingering just beside her cheek. She didn't dare turn to look at him, but her heart screamed he was too close. With her throat tightening, she simply nodded, a faint, soft acknowledgement of his words. Vedha's eyes, however, didn't leave her face. He could see her struggling, fighting the intensity she felt, and it only drew him closer. There was something heartbreakingly beautiful about her innocence, the way her face turned rigid when she tried suppressing her affection for him.

A moment later, he broke the silence again, his voice low and gentle. "Can we go there?"

She turned, finally facing him. His eyes, warm and hopeful, gazed at her, waiting for her answer.

She swallowed hard, her gaze still fixed on the distant sea view. "Hmm?" Vedha smiled a subtle, victorious smile.

"Sir, your Cappucino!" the bearer interrupted, handing him a disposable cup of steaming coffee.

Vedha turned slightly startled and took the cup with a courteous nod, "Thank you".

"Come, we'll go near the waves," Vedha said, casually taking his cappuccino along, as though it was just another regular evening for him. Saira, who was already overwhelmed by his previous words, simply nodded and walked beside him. He walked fast, leading her out of the cafe and as they stepped onto the soft beach sand, the city noises faded behind them, leaving only the sound of crashing waves and distant murmurs of people. They walked in silence for a while. The wind played with Saira's hair and shawl, Vedha occasionally stole glances at her, noticing how effortlessly beautiful she looked even when the chaos of her inner storm was evident on her face.

Halfway through their walk, Vedha extended his cappuccino toward her. "Here. Have some."

Saira glanced at it, hesitating. "You first," she smiled softly. Vedha squinted, pretending to be offended. "You think I'm offering you poison?" Saira Chuckled. He took a long sip, his eyes not leaving hers. "There. Now it's safe," he teased, before extending it toward her again.

Saira hesitated for another second but then slowly took the cup from his hand, brushing her fingers against his. That accidental touch that skin-on-skin contact made her insides somersault, but she held herself together. She took a small sip.

There were several sips of coffee in silence, which comforted them before he balled up the paper cup and flicked his wrist, throwing it with effortless ease. It twirled in the air and landed straight into the dustbin a few feet away without a miss.

Saira hesitated, her voice barely discernible above the constant roar of the waves. "Can I ask you something?" she started, but her gaze locked on the horizon, deliberately avoiding Vedha's eyes. Vedha felt the significance of her tone, his heart tightening in response. "Of course," he answered softly, adjusting his position slightly to face her, allowing her the space to elaborate.

Saira's voice quivered as she expressed herself, her eyes mirroring the inner conflict she felt. "It's not meant to hurt you, but there's a weight I can't quite articulate. My heart feels like its hardening with each moment that brings us closer. Isn't this unjust? Not to society, but to your family, to your wife."

Vedha's expression transformed into a whirlwind of emotions cascading over his face. He opened his mouth to reply, yet left himself speechless with the seriousness of her worries pressing heavily between them.

"I'm extremely sorry for putting you in a place of giving me your explanations", tears trembled down her cheeks. "It's not something out of the blue I asked you now, this has been something I kept pondering and pestering me inside since we started to talk to each other and I can't hold this feeling of guilt…", she shuddered, "The sting of secretly using someone else's possession, the burden of using it without asking, this nagging guilt….I don't know either how to get rid of it or to live with it peacefully", she burst, yet kept walking slowly.

"Saira…" he turned to her with his voice cracked, low and guilt-ridden, "Don't say that. Don't reduce yourself to a crime that was never yours to begin with."

Her tears streamed down heavier now,

"But it is", she screamed, "It is! Every time you look at me the way you do, every time I feel my heart flutter when you say my name, I feel like I'm stepping into a place that was never meant for me. And every night I think about you, I can't help", her voice cracked, her throat parched from the overwhelming heaviness.

"I've been the one willingly walking into this space between you and me. You didn't lure me here. I let myself fall", Vedha replied.

Saira shook her head, swallowing the lump in her throat. "We are not gonna keep doing this, and surefire this must be the final day, yet this part, this week we spent together, is gonna remain uncovered forever, and this kills me inside", she continued crying.

Vedha turned to her with his gaze sharp but tormented, while Saira continued to quiver through her sobs.

"Saira…" his voice barely escaped, raw and strained. His gaze burned into her with a desperate pleading. "Don't do this to us…"

Saira rasped through her sobs, "I couldn't…" and before she could say anything further, she lunged forward and hugged him tight. Without hesitation, his arms found their way around her, wrapping her into the warmest and most secure embrace she had ever felt. She cried all her heart out, her sobs raw and unfiltered, as if each tear was a piece of her burden finally breaking free.

The salt in the air seemed to carry her pain away, dissolving it into the endless night. Vedha held her close with his palms cradling the back of her head. He didn't hush her or ask her to stop. Instead, he let her fall apart in his arms, trusting that she would gather herself when she was ready. Typically, the attitude every woman craves from her man. He waited patiently, his chin resting over her head as she sobbed against his chest. His heart ached, feeling every tremble of her body, but he knew she needed this. She needed to pour out every bit of suffocating tonnage of pain she carried within.

After what felt like long minutes, her sobs started to pace down, not entirely stopping but slowing to faint, hiccupped breaths.

"Saira…" he whispered, his voice calm yet firm. She slowly lifted her gaze, her lashes were still moist and heavy.

Gently, he cradled her face with his palms cupping her cheeks, his thumbs resting beneath her wet, swollen eyes. She looked like a broken glass doll, shattered but still holding herself together. He hated seeing her like this, carrying a grief she didn't deserve.

"Will you listen to what I'm about to say?" he asked, his voice deep and sincere. "With an open mind?" She blinked, puzzled and still gasping through the aftermath of her cry. Her lips trembled as she nodded weakly, "Y-yeah…"

A long pause.

"Can we go sit on the sand and talk?" his voice softened.

She looked into his eyes, searching for an answer she wasn't even sure she wanted to hear at that moment. But she didn't want to resist him now, not after pouring her heart out.

She nodded faintly, "Hmm".

Without a word, Vedha lowered his palm from her cheek and held her hand instead. His fingers curled around hers, firm but tender, as if silently assuring her that he was with her in this suffering. Without another word, they started walking toward the shore where the waves curled and retreated under the dim moonlight. Saira felt the chill of the night air, but the warmth of his hand gripping hers gave her a sense of belonging which she never admitted she craved from him. Vedha hadn't spoken yet. He strolled, matching her pace, allowing her to settle down from the tremble of her previous sobs.

As they walked further away from the crowd and closer to the silent part of the beach, the only sound audible was the crashing waves and the night breeze brushing past their faces. Finally, after reaching a quiet spot, Vedha gently pulled her hand to make her stop. "Here", he gestured to the sand. "Let's sit."

She nodded again, wordless. Together, they lowered themselves onto the cool sand. Saira folded her legs in half with her hands with her fingers clutched tight on her knees. Vedha sat close beside her with their shoulders brushing, and he placed his hands behind on the sand to support his weight.

The beach roared a little louder, the waves splashed against the shore with a restless vigour, and for a moment both of them fell silent.

Vedha exhaled before he broke the silence and sat straight, rubbing his hands to get rid of the sand stuck in them. "Who are you to me, Saira?" he turned towards her. The foamy waves kept dancing onto the shore. Saira turned and blinked in disbelief as he asked the very thing she had queried him in a detailed manner just a few minutes before

He smirked, amused by how blind she was to her divinity. "You are the epitome of what is love, Saira", she mumbled as if he was just trying to distract her from her grieving.

"You are the dawn of love itself, sheer, unconditional, untouched by the worldly strains", he stammered with a desperate need to convey by exactly bringing out what he had in his mind, " You are where love is born…", he fastened, "the sacred flame", he exhaled, "Uff…I can't bring out words for your divinity, Saira, but that is what you, pure, calming light, what the world struggles and fails at…I can taste the words, but I can't feed them into a sentence to you, Saira, but you are the holy high, the divine", he exhaled the breath he had been holding on.

Saira looked at him. Her face was drenched in the salt of her agony, then shadowed with a new intensity of seriousness that she hadn't felt before. It was not because of what he just said about her. It was the realisation that for the first time, Vedha had stripped his walls down and laid himself bare before her because she had never seen him open up like this, not with this rawness and unfiltered vulnerability. His words, his trembled voice, his pain-ridden confession, it was something beyond love, beyond desire.

"Yes, Saira. You showed me unadulterated love, which is free from ill will. There is no domination, there is no possessiveness, and there is no jealousy. Something purer than the love a child receives from the mother. It's more than that, it's godly, Saira", he struggled to explain more than the engineering derivations he had ever lectured on.

Saira kept blinking but tried to understand what his point was. The water pounded the shore with restless energy. He continued.

Vedha's voice quivered as he spoke with his heart weighed down by the storm of emotions he had suppressed for a long time. His gaze didn't break from hers, as if he owed her nothing but the realness and the unfiltered truth.

"There was no domination as to who would overstep into whose boundaries, Saira," he began, his voice soft but heavy. "You accepted me as I was. Without any demands, without any claims, without any conditions. You accepted my boundaries, my realities, even when it meant knowing I belonged to another woman."

Saira's eyes shimmered with tears, and her throat tightened at his words.

"But I was married," Vedha swallowed hard with his jaw clenching. "You knew I was married. You knew you had no possession over me, and still... You loved me. Unconditionally. With no hope, no future and no demands. You just loved me." His voice cracked painfully. "You didn't try to hold me captive. You didn't try to overstep into my life. You didn't interfere at all. You didn't ask me to change my life for you. You just... loved me as I was."

Saira's tears streamed down endlessly. Her heart throbbed hearing the depth of his confession because this was something she never imagined he would say out loud.

"And you know what..." his voice turned shaky, with his hand clutching his knees. "You had no jealousy over another woman whom I belonged to. You showed no bitterness or resentment. You still chose to love me with that void of never being mine." His face twisted in unbearable pain. "You could have cursed my wife. You could have envied her for having a life with me. You could have manipulated me to leave her. But you didn't, Saira. You didn't." His voice cracked into a sob.

Saira shook her head, breaking down as his words pierced through her soul.

"You didn't want to ruin someone else's world to build yours," Vedha rasped. "You had your integrity, your self-respect, and you kept loving me without crossing the lines precisely for what I was and amn't; it's something so godly, Saira." His voice trembled fiercely. "Because how could someone love like that? Without asking for anything in return. Without any hatred. Without possession. Just pure. Pure and boundless love?"

Saira burst into a painful sob, and her body shook at the unbearable weight of his words.

"You gave me all that Saira, the godly love, and you cannot lower yourself feeling the most useless emotion, of being guilty of something you were never the reason for" he took a breath, "You can't do that, I can't take it".

"You can't do that", he repeated to stress how much he meant what he said.

"Most of the time, a parent's love is also conditional, a kind of give and take, but god never offers love on conditions", his eyes widened as he shook his head, "We had a tremendous divine pull, we felt it mutually, but unfortunately we cannot drag it to marriage, a relationship with a commitment of showering love by holding each other's hands and support ourselves for long. But that doesn't make what we have between us low or strange or something, or a sin, Saira. It's more pure than what marriages preach as love to be", he took a breath.

Saira sobbed.

"This is never an incomplete love, Saira. This is fulfilled already, this is divine. In fact, more fulfilled than anything else", he added, "There are men in the military, Saira," his voice cracked, "Married men. They leave their wives for years. For years. They don't wake up together. They don't have dinner together. They don't sleep in each other's arms. And still, their love doesn't die. It doesn't reduce its depth. It doesn't lose its warmth." He exhaled heavily.

"Why?" his voice rasped now, his chest burning with the heaviness of his confession. "Because their love never relied on proximity. Their love didn't depend on waking up next to each other. Their love didn't demand the constant reassurance of 'I need you beside me'. It was built purely on devotion, patience and unconditionality, and would you dare to say that their love is incomplete because they don't have access to each other every single day, Saira?"

Saira clutched her chest with her tears choking her now.

Vedha turned his face towards her, his gaze dark, honest, and tormented. "Saira, what you and I have", his voice broke, "is that kind of love. And if I hadn't met you, I would have never known what pure love is. I would've gone my whole life being a husband who thought he was loving when in reality, he was owning. Maybe possessive too"

Saira's body trembled uncontrollably now, her mind unable to grasp the weight of what he had just confessed. Vedha let out a painful, bitter laugh. "And the irony, Saira?" his eyes welled up. "I had to meet you outside my marriage to learn what true love feels like."

Saira gasped painfully, her sobs now wrenching through her throat. Vedha's throat tightened with his heart heavy with the weight of fate's cruelty. His voice lowered, carrying the burden of helplessness. "And to fight against destiny..." he began, his voice cracking, "is pointless, Saira."

Saira looked at him, her tear-soaked face still etched with longing and heartbreak.

"Yes, it pains..." he exhaled, his gaze distant, "it aches... it crumbles every inch of your soul. And yet," his voice trembled, "we still exist, Saira"

Saira's lips quivered, her hands clutching her knees.

Vedha smiled bitterly, his voice now drowned in despair. "Maybe that's the whole point, Saira. Maybe that's the only task fate has given us ... to overcome this pain, this suffering and still exist. Grieve and still exist"

A deep silence fell between them, with only the sound of the crashing waves filling the void.

"And maybe..." Vedha's voice cracked, his words tasting like poison, "Maybe that's exactly why we couldn't end up being married."

Saira gasped audibly, her eyes widening in shock.

Vedha laughed bitterly, his face twisted with agony. "I'm sure, I'm damn sure that what we have between us is not an ordinary feeling, Saira. Like just another feeling we share with anyone in this life. If it is not ordinary, it must be transcendental, isn't it? It's the kind of love that destroys you, rips you apart, and still doesn't die." His voice cracked, "It's the kind of love that the universe can't afford to let thrive in a marriage".

Tears flooded Saira's face as she helplessly watched him struggle with his pain.

Vedha smiled painfully, his jaw clenched. "Because if we had ended up together, Saira..." his throat tightened, "the world wouldn't have known the difference between possessive love and pure love. Our love would've been caged in societal definitions. It would've lost its divinity the moment it gained a title."

A painful sob escaped Saira's throat, and Vedha immediately turned to her, his eyes burning with unspoken sorrow. "Maybe that's why fate pulled us apart..." his voice broke, "because the universe knew that the kind of love we share. It's meant to be felt, not possessed. It's meant to transcend, not settle. It's meant to remain pure, not claimed."

Saira's face contorted with unbearable pain with her chest heaving like a mountain. Vedha exhaled heavily, his voice now completely torn. "And maybe..." he whispered, his eyes welling up, "maybe the biggest proof of our love... is that we couldn't end up together."

A soul-crushing silence enveloped them.

"Because what we have…" Vedha's voice cracked one last time, "is the love that cannot be measured in a marriage certificate, nor societal norms." His voice shook, "It's the love that could only stay untainted, yet can remain fulfilled" he pulled her hand that clutched her knee and placed it on his right palm and closed with his left palm, holding it tight. Saira leaned her head on his shoulders with tears trembling in her eyes, but her gaze never withdrew from the horizon. That moment shattered them both. But then their realisation leapt to another level with their understanding that their love was never destined to be lived, but it was destined to remain divine.

Her silence pestered him more, with just the crashing waves filling the void between them and their growing ache. He turned to her with his voice barely above a whisper. "Saira…" She did not move and sat still looking at the restless sea as if it had all the answers in its endless depth. The ocean always had answers we were ignorant of hearing. The hush of waves, the way they kiss the shore only to retreat at every wind that flew along, the restless rhythm that never ceased, always carried the answers, we just never listened.

"Saira…" he called again. "Say something…" his voice wavered, "Please". She remained the same with her head slightly on his shoulders, and exhaled. "I have always felt how beautiful it is…" she said in a low tone.

"What…" he queried softly without any understanding of what she was trying to say.

"That one..." she pointed her fingers to the horizon. He blinked in confusion, unsure of how the conversation had taken this detour.

"I have always felt how beautiful it is. The way the horizon exists..." She tried hard to continue, yet she did.

"The line where the sky and ocean meet, it looks like they meet" Tears trembled again. "But, in reality, they never meet. And they cannot meet. Just like us, so close, so connected yet, destined to stay apart".

Vedha is shocked by the depth and clenches his jaws.

"It looks beautiful and complete from the outside, to see from here. But the pain", she cried heavily with her words faltering as another wave of sobs escaped her.

He followed her gaze to the horizon, where the sky and sea stretched into infinity, appearing to meet, yet forever apart. It was the cruelly poetic reply she could ever give him for all the explanations he gave himself and her. He swallowed hard, realising that no philosophy, no wisdom, no justification could erase the sting of separation she was feeling. The ache and the longing were real. And despite everything, the pain was still the pain that couldn't be escaped. He held her fingers tight as if the only truth that mattered at that moment was her presence and her pain that mirrored his own. The sorrow he suppressed in his chest broke free as tears buried in the dark. The ocean continued to roar, indifferent to their heartbreak, like it had seen a thousand such stories before.

He did not speak a word. Moreover, there was nothing left to explain. There was nothing left to justify, and he let his tears answer the pain; neither of them knew why they were suffering. Sometimes the solution to any problem is just to cry out and surrender. She remained leaning on his shoulder while his head rested gently against hers. Their hands remained locked with their fingers intertwined as if letting go would shatter the fragile moment holding them together. The waves whispered secrets neither of them could understand, yet somehow they felt heard. Beneath the infinite blue where time seemed to blur, they sat with blurry eyes gazing at the place where the sky and sea pretended to meet just like them.

"I love you, Saira", Vedha gently pulled back, turning towards her.

"I love you so much, Vedha" Her stare held his, unshaken and intense.

Vedha exhaled softly, "Saira..." he murmured, tilting his head slightly toward her, "Tell me something beyond me, beyond us. Something you wish for in your life, Saira?"

She stirred against his shoulders, blinking away the mist in her eyes. "Why?" she asked with a voice barely above a whisper.

"If it's within my best possibility, I want to give it to you." he said, tightening his grip on her hand. The thought of him wanting to fulfil a wish of hers, despite their impossible fate, made her chest tighten. She hesitated, gathering her thoughts. The truth was, there were many things she had wished for, some had been buried, and some still longed for. But, in that moment, she wasn't sure of what she could say that wouldn't make his heart ache even more.

Saira's lip parted, but no elaborate wish came forth. She sighed and whispered, "Nothing", with an elegant smile. "Nothing?" he repeated with his brows knitting in confusion. She shook her head, gripping his hand tighter. "Just…this", she admitted. "You're beside me in this moment, in my pain, not making me feel like I have to silence everything I feel. This is enough", she said.

Vedha swallowed hard, he had expected a wish that was tangible that he could make happen, something he could control. Her fingers traced over a metal, feeling the carved letters beneath her thumb. The coldness of the ring contrasted sharply with the warmth of his palm.

"Ishu", Vedha murmured before she could ask. She did not ask further. She knew it had to be his wife. The woman he was bound to by vows, fate, and everything that made her existence in his life feel like a forbidden dream. She did not pull her hand away, but she did not press further either. She just let it be. A sorrowful chuckle slipped past her lips like an attempt to mask the ache swelling inside her.

"Don't worry", she exhaled, looking ahead at the restless waves. "Just for now, I knew I couldn't wish for the same forever" Her voice held acceptance but also the quiet shattering pain of knowing that some things are never meant to last. Silence hung between them, stretching like the horizon before them. Endless and inevitable.

Saira's phone buzzed in her jean pocket, breaking the silence between them. She frowned, wondering who would be calling her at this hour. For a brief moment, her heart pounded with fear: "Had the hostel staff found out I was missing?" This thought sent a cold shiver down her spine. The name flashing on the screen made her pause. Anya.

But then a glance at Vedha steadied her nerves. He gave an assuring nod. A silent signal to pick up the call. She swiped to answer.

"Saira", heard the voice.

"Anya, did they find out?" Saira asked in fear.

"Who knows…?" Anya's voice remained casual, but there was a hint of curiosity bound with care, "But, where are you?"

Saira hesitated for a moment before replying, "At the beach". "The beach?" Anya repeated, a little surprised.

"Yes, Anya", Saira confirmed softly.

A brief silence followed, and then Anya's voice lowered with concern. "All good?" You are fine, right?"

Saira glanced at Vedha. His gaze was steady on her, his presence unwavering. "Yes, he is with me", she said what she said. There was another pause. "Okay, call me if you need any help. I'll be just a call away".

Saira smiled faintly, "I know. Thank you, Anya".

As the call ended, she stared at the screen for a moment. It was already 2 AM, and the glow of her phone illuminated her face in the dark. Vedha noted the time and then watched her with his calm voice. "She cares about you".

Saira nodded, pocketing her phone. "She does".

Vedha softly insisted again, carrying both urgency and tenderness in his voice and constant gaze at her, searching for an answer beyond her 'This is enough'.

"Saira", he murmured, tightening his grip on her hands. "Tell me something for my happiness. What do you want?"

His words hung in the air with their heaviness upon the desperate attempt to give her something or anything in a situation where fate had denied them so much. Saira looked down with her lips parting as if to speak, yet no words came. She wondered what she could ask for in a reality where they were caught in this cruel, inescapable fate. Saira exhaled deeply, trying to push away the ache in her throat and then, deciding at that very moment, she lifted her gaze back to him, and a faint melancholic smile touched her lips.

"Take me on a bike ride", she whispered, "A little fast".

Vedha studied her for a second, but his expression was unreadable. Then, without another word, he took her hand and got up from the sand, brushing off the grains that clung to his clothes. Vedha walked ahead to the cafe quickly. He paid the bill, collected the paper bag and walked towards his bike while Saira followed him with her lighter steps.

Vedha revved the engine with a deep roar, slicing through the stillness of the night to engrave this moment into the time itself, something he wanted to echo in their memories whenever life allowed them to feel it again. Saira hopped onto the seat behind him with her legs apart, settling into the familiar space. Without any hesitation, her hand found his right shoulder with the warmth of his body grounding her. The touch that held more meaning beyond just words, like a trust and a sense of belonging, even in a love that wasn't meant to be. He inhaled sharply, steadying himself, and then, without another word, he twisted the throttle and the bike surged forward, carrying them into the wind, into the night, into another fleeting escape from reality.

As the breeze rushed against her face, she tilted her head slightly, surrendering to its embrace. She inhaled deeply, trying to trap the moisture of the night air within her lungs along with the memory of this moment, feeling his presence and the quiet intimacy of their closeness. Slowly, she withdrew her hand from his shoulder, hesitating for just a moment before wrapping both her arms around him from behind. The warmth of his body felt steady and reassuring, like an anchor in that fleeting night. As she leaned forward, her head found its place against his back, pressing her ear against his back just below his neck. She closed her eyes, letting the rhythm of his breathing sync with hers, feeling the gentle rise and fall of his chest beneath her cheek. Vedha tapped gently a couple of times on the back of her palm like an acknowledgement of her gentle yet tight hug. He smiled in the front, a rare, genuine smile that he didn't have to suppress this time. He allowed himself to enjoy the moment and feel her warmth pressed against his back, the way her arms fit around his chest. As the bike sped forward, cutting through the cool night air, he did not feel the need to rush anywhere. The road stretched ahead, unknown and uncertain, yet at that moment, he let himself believe that maybe, just maybe, time had frozen just for them.

Vedha jerked a little when Saira suddenly tapped his shoulder and said, "Stop, stop!" in an urgency. His immediate thought was that if something went wrong, perhaps she felt uncomfortable or had an issue with the speed of the ride. Without thinking further, he hit the brakes smoothly and turned his head back to check on her. But before he could ask, she grinned mischievously. "Can I drive now?"

Vedha turned back and blinked in surprise, "Oh? You know how to?" "No", she admitted with a wide grin.

He raised an eyebrow. "And?"

"You will sit behind me", she stated, her eyes twinkling with excitement.

A chuckle escaped his lips before he could suppress it. He wasn't expecting this playful demand from her, like a sudden shift of energy that made him feel a blush creep up on his face. Shaking his head, he sighed in surrender. "Alright, alright", he said, stepping off the bike.

As she slid forward onto the rider's seat, he swung his leg over and took his place behind her. She gripped the handlebars, and her confidence was unwavering despite her inexperience. She turned back and nodded her head, pointing her hand at the handlebars, signalling him to hold her hands and take charge of the ride now. Vedha smirked out of blush and held her hands above the handlebars.

As he twisted the accelerator, the bike hummed beneath them, surging forward smoothly. Saira felt a rush of excitement, but this time not from the speed alone but the way they were closer than before. His breath was near her ear, this presence pressed against her back, and his hands were along her hands with palms held tighter on the handlebars, and the moment felt intoxicating to her. She barely paid attention to the ride because the truth was, Vedha was still the one in control, guiding the bike effortlessly from behind while letting her revel in the illusion of handling it. Her gaze flickered to the rearview mirror, and there they were, their faces impossibly close, framed together as if they belonged. Her lips curled into a soft smile at the sight.

Vedha noticed her reaction with his grip steady on the handles. Though he was enjoying the moment too, his mind remained alert, ensuring they stayed safe.

"Eyes on the road, Saira", he murmured near her ear with his voice both teasing and careful. She chuckled, biting her lip, "Okies, Professor Vedha".

Vedha smirked a smile but did not respond. The night breeze carried their laughter as the bike glided forward, and for her, nothing else in the world mattered at that moment.

After riding for enough minutes, they finally pulled over at a small roadside shop where the neon light flickered above, casting a dim glow on the quiet street. Vedha stepped inside and returned with a bottle of water. He twisted the cap open before handing it to Saira. She took a few sips, just enough to refresh herself and then wordlessly extended the bottle back to him. Vedha drank deeply, and as the cool water eased the dryness in his throat, he splashed some over his face. Droplets trickled down his jaw as he wiped his face with his palm, inhaling the crisp night air.

Saira watched him throwing a thoughtful gaze, "Feeling sleepy?" she asked softly.

Vedha turned to her with an undecipherable expression at first, and then a faint smirk curved his lips. "You are beside me for the one last night", he said with a low and steady voice, "would I even wish to sleep?" he said, dabbing his face with his kerchief.

His words stuck with her like a sudden gust of wind. Her fingers instinctively curled into her palm, thinking, "It's only tonight. This night is the eleventh hour. The last fleeting moment before the inevitable", she thought. Her heart twisted inside her chest, although she had known all along that their time was borrowed like a delicate sandcastle by the shore, waiting for the tide to sweep it away. And yet, hearing aloud like a snoozed alarm made it all too real. She remained silent for his reply.

Vedha twisted the cap back onto the bottle and tossed it into the nearby dustbin. As he turned back, his eyes caught Saira's distant expression, noticing the way she stood with her eyebrows knitted together and lost in thought.

"Hmm, but let's not ruin this night by thinking about tomorrow", he said, trying to anchor her back into the moment.

Saira blinked and looked up at him, and tilted her head slightly. "What now?" she asked, forcing a small smile.

"Another ride?" he asked with a wink and nodded toward the bike.

"No…. something slow", she muttered as if she was speaking more to time itself than to him. Vedha narrowed his eyes playfully, "Eh?", and sought confirmation.

She looked up at him and with quiet certainty she said, "We will walk".

Vedha stole a glance at her. He knew that this wasn't just about walking, and she wanted to slow down time to hold on to this night before reality came crashing in. A small knowing smile tugged at his lips, "Alright then", he said, extending his hand toward her, "Let's walk".

It was a quiet night where the air trembled with the slow, sultry murmur of restless creatures and their song thick with desire. Their fingers intertwined as they walked down the empty street, the neon glow from the street lamps casting long and soft shadows behind them. Saira tilted her head toward him and broke the silence, "Hmm, tell me your favourites", she said with her voice light but playful.

Vedha turned to look at her with his lips curling into a knowing smile. "No", he said, although the warmth of his eyes betrayed the amusement he tried to hide. Saira urged again, "Come on".

Vedha chuckled, shaking his head, "Why would you want to know?" he asked, raising a brow. "Simply", she shrugged with her eyes twinkling under the streetlights.

He let out a soft sigh, looking straight ahead, "I won't", he murmured. Saira frowned slightly with her steps slowing, "Why?"

A pause.

Saira did not feel like pressing further, although she did not understand why he refused to share. She exhaled and remained quiet.

"Promise me", he broke the silence this time. She remained silent.

"Promise me that someday you will marry someone for your life," Vedha said with a voice steady yet gentle like a quiet plea wrapped in inevitability.

Saira felt a jolt in her chest as if he had reached into her soul and grasped the very ache she had tried to suppress. She wondered how he was always able to articulate the thoughts she hadn't even voiced. She turned to look at him with her eyes searching his.

"You can't live your life in the memories of us forever, Saira," he continued with his tone firm yet aching. "Life has to move on".

She swallowed hard one more time.

"I can tell you my favourites," he added, "but only if you promise me that you're only dwelling in them for a while, but not forever"

The weight of his words crashed over her like a wave. The future he spoke of, the one where she was supposed to move on, felt like an unbearable void. A world where she would no longer have him to hold onto for her life. Tears welled up in her eyes, spilling over before she could even attempt to stop them, shuddering the sorrow she had been trying to contain.

Vedha wanted to hold her, to erase her pain, but he knew that some wounds had to be felt before they could heal.

"You can easily tell me to move on, but do you know what it took for me to stand here and hear you say that, Vedha sir?" She looked into his eyes, searching for something or anything that would tell her that he understood. She continued, "The pain…the way it crumbled me from within knowing that no matter how much I loved you, this was never meant to be….", he voice cracked yet she managed, "Only I knew what it felt like to wake up every day blaming the fate, blaming my bad luck and blaming my existence on this earth to have all these happened to me"

His throat tightened with unspoken agony, "Do you think it's not painful to me, Saira?" His voice was raw,

"Yes, this happened, we don't know why. But what I'm saying is we can't keep clinging to it".

She looked at him with teary eyes, "Clinging?" she whispered, almost as if the word itself cut her.

"Clinging on to how we spend time together, the words we spoke, the breath we shared, the hug, the cappuccino, this beach, the ride, this night", he lifted their palms held together and showed, "this walk", he smiled and "my favourites", he paused.

Saira looked away, pressing her lips together. A long pause.

"Saira…" she softly called, stepping a little closer. She did not respond. He continued after a pause.

"Okay, can I say something of my extreme favourite that I wouldn't mind you clinging on to for the rest of your life?" His words were slow and deliberate.

Saira's curiosity flickered instantly with an eye slightly widened, building an anticipation within. Favourite food? Favourite book? Favourite author? Favourite movie? Or what was it to binge with? Her mind crossed through all the questions she had prepared herself to ask him. It took her a second to realise that he wasn't going to say it unless she asked for it, unless she showed him that she truly wanted to hear it. Yet, she refused to ask, making him know that she was still carrying a little anger and frustration with his 'Life has to move on' advice. Still, she wanted him to say.

He still lifted his brows and signalled if she wanted to know. She signalled him back, raising her brow and asking him what that was.

He turned to her slowly and deliberately. And lowered his head just enough to be close, closer than he had ever allowed himself before, with his gaze locked onto hers deep and unwavering. For a moment, the world around him blurred, the street lights flickered in the distance with the faint rustle of the wind brushing past them. But all she could see was him and his eyes. And then with a voice barely above a whisper, yet heavy with meaning, he spoke.

"You". One word. She understood the truth, yet, surrendering to the intensity of the moment, she chose to mask it, turning it into something playful, as if her heart wasn't shattering and soaring at the same time.

She wriggled out of his hold, she shoved his hand away from hers with a mischievous spark flashing in her tears. "You... Hopeless trickster", she huffed with her lips curling into a half- smile as she took a step back. Vedha raised an eyebrow in confusion for a split second before he saw the glint in her eyes, the way her emotions danced between pain and playfulness. But before he could react, she turned on her heels and bolted with her eyes darting around searching for something for a twig or a pebble to grab and playfully hit him with.

"Saira!" he called out, but she was already running with her laughter breaking through the heavy silence of the night. And then with an exasperated chuckle, Vedha ran before she could chase him. Their footsteps echoed in the empty street. He turned back mid-run, grinning at her, but before he could react, she reached out and caught him. In one swift motion, she flung her arms around him, holding him tight as if capturing a moment she never wanted to let go of. Their breaths were ragged, and their bodies radiated warmth from the chase. Just two of them, wrapped in each other's arms, stood still in a love that never needed any description or validation.

As they remained in the embrace, neither of them moved as if they feared that even the slightest shift would break the fragile moment. Vedha gently pulled back just enough to look into her eyes. His gaze was steady, filled with the softness that carried both infinite love and indelible sorrow. He held her shoulders tightly and in a firm tone, "I need you to get married, Saira".

Stiffened in his hold, Saira's brows knitted together, but he didn't let her react just yet.

"I need you to experience everything", he continued. "The whole point of life is to experience. We…." he paused and exhaled before pressing forward, "We cannot end up together because we did not feel it any time soon. And we would never choose to do anything against it, but it doesn't necessarily mean that you should not allow yourself to move on" he paused.

Her breath hitched, and he caught the flicker of pain in her eyes.

"Do you get what I'm saying, Saira?" he shook her shoulders with his tone filled with quiet urgency.

"Moving on doesn't mean you loved me any less", he said. With his hands still resting on her shoulders as if grounding her, "To move on from whatever that wrecked us… that is the strength, and I want my Saira to embrace that strength, to build it, to live by it".

Her breath trembled, and he saw her eyes portraying the war between holding on and letting go.

"If you do that", he whispered, "then our love…it succeeds every single time"

Tears slipped down her cheek, but she didn't wipe them away, because, for the first time, she saw love in a way she never had before. The weight of his words sank deep into her bones. She wanted to protest, to argue that love shouldn't be something one had to be strong enough to walk away from. But deep down, she knew Vedha was right.

"Our love will live on in every choice you make for yourself, every joy you allow yourself, in every moment you embrace instead of mourn."

He lifted her chin slightly, making her look at him for one more time. "Promise me", he pulled her hand and pressed her palm on his chest, "Promise me that you will make our love thrive in your life forever".

Saira exhaled with tears slipping down her cheeks, with her hand feeling his heartbeat, she whispered, "I promise…" she cried heavily yet managed to say again, "I promise I won't let it fade".

"Probably, the one real 'forever' promise between the lovers", he teased with a playful glint in his eyes and wiped away the tear lingering on her cheek.

Saira scoffed, half-amused and half-teary-eyed, "That sounds like Vedha-style love philosophy"

"Call it whatever you want", he smirked and winked. She smiled.

They held each other's hands and walked towards the bike with their slow, unhurried steps. With each step they walked forward, it felt like they untangled the knots of suffering, proving that pain, like time, fades in motion, but the only thing we must do is to keep moving on without letting ourselves be trapped in the wreckage of the past. A weight lifted off her soul, as guilt slowly unravelled its grip on her. She understood that it was the very fact that they walked together, holding each other for that period in their lives, while they were bound by the same pain and suffering that had shattered them like never before. As they walked, they looked like living proof of life's inevitable wreckage, embodying the truth that the only way out of pain is 'through it'.

And there, up in the vast expanse of the night sky, two stars gleamed a little brighter as if whispering the same story they had lived. Perhaps, the universe has always known that love like theirs was never meant to fade, only to transform. Their love radiated just like those stars which burned at a distance quietly in the void that was not despite the darkness but because of it.

They reached the bike and with a swift motion, Vedha kicked it to life. The quiet hum of the engine blended with the night's hush. Saira picked up the paper bag resting on the engine before she hopped onto the seat behind him. As she settled in, her hands found their place on his shoulder in a silent understanding. The warmth of the moment wrapped around them as he eased the bike forward, gliding through the empty roads.

The breeze felt different now, not just air rushing past, but signifying it was always about what we feel inside that reflects outside, something deeper and cleansing. It carried away the weight they had held, whispering that love was not only in holding on but in the grace of letting go. With every breath, they both embraced the feeling of the beauty of now, allowing the night to weave its final pages.

Finally, they arrived at the hostel road in quiet peace around 4 AM. The once-familiar path now felt not as a place of restriction, but as a witness to something profound. Saira no longer feared being caught, such worries were forfeited and turned insignificant against the vastness of what she had just lived, a reckoning night that allowed her the silent mendings of wounds neither of them had words for. And that she knew was worth everything she risked.

As she stepped down from the bike, she gently handed the paper bag to Vedha.

"Thanks, Saira", he said, "Not just for the dress, but for trusting me and allowing me to be the one you leaned on, even if only for one last time."

She met his gaze, her voice was soft yet uncertain. "I should be the one thanking you", she said, "Not just for my safety, but for the way you had held space for my pain and the unspoken understanding between us". They filled the air with gratitude for the profound healing they had given each other without expectations, with just the raw truth of what they had been and what they could never be.

Vedha's eyes flickered toward the chai shop, where the old watchman sat engrossed in his newspaper, the dim glow of the shop's lantern casting shadows over his wrinkled face. The hostel gate stood ajar, swaying slightly in the night breeze, as if fate itself had left a passage open for her.

Vedha glanced at the watchman once again and turned to Saira, "You go in. I will handle him", he said in a low voice. Saira hesitated for a second, her eyes searching his as if wanting to hold on just a little longer. But, she knew he was right, she nodded and took a step toward the hostel gate, her heart pounding not out of fear, but the weight of goodbye.

Vedha walked towards the tea shop and watched her back for a moment before turning toward the tea shop. He walked in casually with his fingers tightening around the paper bag. "One chai", he said to the vendor and slid onto the stool, pretending like this was just an ordinary night, although nothing about this night had been ordinary.

Saira hurried inside with light footsteps, but urgently. She climbed the stairs with her heart racing with the heaviness of overwhelming emotions. As she reached her room, she swiftly unlocked the door and stepped in, closing it behind her with a deep exhale. Without a second thought, she rushed to the window, pulling the curtains aside just enough to peek through.

From there, she had a clear view of the tea shop across the street. Her eyes searched for Vedha. There, he was sitting in the corner, holding a cup of chai with his relaxed, unaware posture. The watchman flipping through his newspaper barely paid him any attention. She exhaled softly, assuring he had handled it.

Saira picked up her phone and dialled his number with her fingers trembling slightly with the strange ache of farewell. Vedha answered on the first ring. "You reached safely?" he asked with his voice low yet gentle.

"Yes", she whispered while her eyes fixed on him from the window. "I'm watching you".

At that, Vedha lifted his gaze from his tea and turned toward her window as if he had already known she was there. A small, knowing smile played on his lips. He did not utter a word, but his eyes held hers across the distance, silent yet speaking volumes. Vedha took a slow sip of his tea and then exhaled as if trying to release something heavy from within, but his gaze remained locked with hers through the dimly lit street.

"Take care, Saira", he said with his voice steady, yet carrying the weight of unspoken emotions. She gripped the phone tightly as she tried to ground herself in the reality of letting go of him.

"And…" he hesitated for a second and continued, "Whenever you think of me, remember the promise you made".

Her breath hitched, recollecting the promise she made to him, to live, to move forward and not let their love be a cage but a strength. She nodded slowly, even though he could barely see it, "I will", she whispered.

There was silence on the other end for a brief moment, and her voice came through, steady but heavy, "Bye Vedha".

"Bye, Saira", he told back with equal heaviness as hers. He let the words linger for a second before pressing the end button. As soon as the call disconnected, he let out a deep breath which he had been holding for a long time. Just then, the watchman turned from his spot at the tea shop, folding the newspaper as he noticed Vedha still sitting there. With curiosity in his eyes, he asked, "Waiting for someone?"

Vedha, steadying his emotions, shook his head with a small smile. "No..I just came to drop my wife off for the journey she was supposed to take".

The old man chuckled adjusting his pants as he walked closer to Vedha, "Oh I see, it's difficult until she comes back", he gave a lengthy cackle and said, "Wife-less life is messy", he gave Vedha a knowing nod, placing a rough yet, comforting hand on his shoulder, "Take care, brother".

Vedha simply smiled in return, a kind of smile that held a story too deep to be spoken aloud. As the watchman strolled towards the hostel gate, Vedha's gaze momentarily followed him before he whispered under his breath, "She won't come back…it's her journey".

He walked towards his bike, his fingers brushing over the handle as if grounding himself in reality. The night air was thick with a strange kind of stillness, the one that comes when something truly ends. With a swift motion, he swung his leg over the bike, gripping the handles firmly. The streetlights above flickered for a moment, casting long shadows on the empty road ahead. He gave a last glance at the window that was closed with curtains and moved forward.

Saira stood still behind the curtains, allowing herself to drown in the heaviness for a while and then texted back to Anya that she had reached the room. She then lay on the bed and dozed off.

# DAY 7: The Last Echo

She slept for a solid two hours with her body resting and her mind drifting between dreams and reality. She woke up at 6.30 AM. There was no heaviness in her eyes, yet no complete freshness in her soul either. It was as if the night had left traces of itself within her, the memories that hadn't settled and emotions that hadn't faded.

She sat on the bed for a moment, staring at the soft morning light seeping through the curtains, hitting her with the realisation that the world outside had moved forward, as it always did. The birds sang, the streets began to hum with life, and the city slowly stretched itself awake despite the long dark hours.

She inhaled deeply, then exhaled, grounding herself to the present. Today wasn't another day of her college, not another routine, not another normalcy to step into, it wasn't just another day because it was Vedha's last working day in the college. It lingered like a quiet awareness to her. Rising from the bed, she moved through her morning routine with mechanical ease, brushing her hair, adjusting her kurta, and slipping on her sandals. Every action felt like preparing herself not just for college but for the inevitable.

By the time she was ready, the clock ticked forward, but indifferent to what the day meant for her. With a steady breath, she picked up her bag, slung it over her shoulder, and stepped out, walking towards the day that waited for her. As she stepped onto the college bus, she noticed everything around her operated as if nothing had changed. The familiar rumbling of the engine, the quiet chatter of students, and the routine stops all along the way to college.

As the bus slowly rolled into the college premises, her eyes instinctively searched for him. And there he was, already at the bike stand, parking his bike with the same effortless ease as any other day. She watched him with her heart swelling with something deeper than love. Respect, admiration and a silent gratitude that only she could understand.

Despite the weight of the night they had shared, despite the storm of emotions they had both braved, he stood there as if untouched by it. And she now knew that it wasn't because he was unaffected, but he had chosen to carry it differently. He wasn't the kind of man who only spoke of strength. He lived it. He did not just tell her to move forward; he embodied it, showing up even when it hurt, standing tall even when the weight was unbearable.

And at that moment, Saira felt proud. Proud of the man she had fallen in love with. Proud that her heart had chosen someone who not only understood her pain but carried it with her, walking beside her through it. Someone who didn't just offer comforting words but gave her the kind of strength she needed, spoke in the language of her soul, in the way she needed to hear it most. Before he could turn, the bus moved forward, carrying her away from him. She exhaled softly, stepped off the bus and blended into the students making their way to the respective blocks, her feet moving with her familiarity with routine.

As she entered her classroom, she immediately spotted Anya, who had been waiting for her. Anya waited for Saira to settle in, watching her closely, trying to gauge the emotions lingering beneath her calm demeanour, just like best friends. Saira adjusted her bag, exhaled softly and then turned to her friend, "Hi, Anya".

Anya smirked, "Hi, madam, so…how was last night?"

Saira leaned back slightly with a distant look passing over her face before she smiled. A smile that carried both the weight and warmth of everything that had transpired.

Saira exhaled, depicting the impact it had done on her, "Heavy..." she admitted, "But beautiful….beautiful enough to hold on to for life".

Anya tilted her head, studying her. Then, with a slow nod, she grinned, "Awesome".

Anya needed no further explanation. She understood that sometimes it takes just a few hours for life to change forever. Moreover, she anticipated something like this for Saira and probably why she had encouraged her to talk to Vedha even when Saira was confused about letting her feelings grow with a married man. This closure or this clarity or whatever Saira had felt is what Anya wanted her to gain, too. Now, on hearing the fulfilment in Saira's voice, Anya felt assured. She stood by her friend in difficult times, believing in her integrity and strength and no wonder, she felt proud of that choice of hers too.

The long and seemingly never-ending lectures finally passed, and the evening arrived once again. As Saira occupied her usual corner in the bus, a soft breeze touched her face, despite the golden rays of the dusking sun spreading its warmth across the sky. The air felt different; it was not heavy, and it was not suffocating. It was light, carrying a sense of serene closure.

The usual chaos of students filled the bus, their voices blended into a familiar hum, yet the same window seat that had once stirred flutters in her heart and left her with an inexplicable ache just days ago, now gave her something else, turning her turbulent, compelling acceptance into a calm, mature acceptance. She had a deep breath that did not hurt her anymore. She saw him walking along the pedestal with his backpack slung over one shoulder and the helmet in his hand. His pace was steady and unhurried as if carrying the weight of finality with quiet grace. Just then, he paused to shake with a professor, perhaps someone wishing him well for the journey ahead, for the future he was about to step into.

For a fleeting moment, it felt surreal. That walk with his lone silhouette against the golden dusk seemed like a scene from a dream. Another dream she had lived for real, like a life she had wished and lived the last night with him. Although it had a quiet ache, it was still something beautiful passing into memory. His eyes found hers across the distance, and in that fleeting second, a familiar warmth passed between them. He smiled, a soft knowing unburdened smile. The kind of smile that didn't ask for anything, it did not hold on to anything, yet carried a sparkle. It wasn't the kind of gaze that stole her breath away or made her chest clench with longing. It was calmer, almost like the endless sea when the storm had passed, deep, steady and at peace with itself.

She smiled back, not as someone clinging to what was, but as someone carrying it forward like a gentle tide taking the remnants of a wave and folding them into the ocean. He walked ahead with the same quiet smile with his steps neither rushed nor hesitant, as if he had already made peace with the weight he once carried. As he reached the bike stand, he swung his backpack over his shoulder, slid the helmet on and with one swift motion, brought the engine to life.

The roar of the engine cut through the evening air, not with the aching sorrow of departure like before, but with a bold and unspoken declaration. A noisy proclamation that life doesn't pause, that time doesn't wait, that no matter how deep the love, how bittersweet the farewell, the wheels must keep turning.

And as he rode away, the sound of the engine faded into the horizon, leaving only the echo of a chapter well-lived, a love well felt, and the certainty that life in all its impermanence must move forward.

Saira leaned back against the seat, letting the wind brush against her face as she gulped down the ache that carried both the weight of longing and the strange comfort of having lived it, even if it's just for a moment. She exhaled a bittersweet smile ghosting her lips and whispered to herself,

"To the love that never was, but always will be. Yours painfully, until I learned to be mine"

And with that, she closed her eyes for a fleeting second, allowing the words to settle in her soul, not a wound, but as wisdom.

The bus jolted forward, merging into the stream of life that never stopped for anyone. Saira let herself sink into the motion, feeling the weight in her heart shift, not vanishing, but finding a place to rest. The wind rushed past her window, carrying with it echoes of laughter, unspoken words and a love that was never meant to stay, only meant to be felt.

# BEYOND EXISTENCE

6 years later.

The sound of applause rippled through the hall, growing louder as the audience rose to their feet in a standing ovation. It was another moment she had never truly envisioned for herself, yet here she was. Saira, standing at the podium with the microphone in hand, faced a sea of admiration. She had just finished answering a question about her journey, about the words that once weighed heavily in her heart, now finding their place on the pages of a book that had left a mark on many hearts, stirring their emotions far and wide.

For a brief second, her eyes scanned the crowd, half expecting to catch a familiar gaze from the past, but instead, her heart anchored to the present. There he was, her husband, standing amidst the applause, holding their child in his arms, capturing the moment on his phone with his eyes gleaming with pride, reflecting a love that had witnessed her journey from the shadows of heartbreak to the brilliance of her purpose.

She smiled with utmost steadiness and certainty, as she leaned closer to the mike, "This book is not just mine", she said, "It belongs to every heart that has ever loved deeply, lost completely and dared to find itself again".

Another grand round of applause.

Sometimes we find ourselves questioning the life events that unfold, wondering why certain things happen to us despite our deepest wishes. We may carry regrets, dwelling on the choices we hadn't made or blaming ourselves for walking paths we never intended to tread.

Saira, too, once resented the course of her life, choosing engineering, a path she never desired. She thought it was a detour, a compromise, a sacrifice of her dreams. But engineering, the very thing she initially resisted, became the spark that illuminated her passion. It wasn't just the path itself but the journey through it that shaped her. It gave her experiences, stories and resilience, the raw material for the storyteller she was always meant to become. That's life, in its mysterious ways, often places us exactly where we need to be, not where we want to be. Even when it feels like we're being led astray, we are in some unseen way being guided home.

We are not merely bodies moving through time. We are the stories, unfolding in the hearts of those we meet, echoes in the lives we touch. Every kindness extended, every truth shared, and every love given without conditions are the invisible threads that weave the world into something whole. Perhaps, the most beautiful thing is that we may never fully see the extent of our impact, and never witness all the ways we help mend what was once broken. But somewhere, in the vastness of existence, someone's life becomes lighter because we are here. And that is enough. That is everything.

*Dedicated to every Vedha and Saira out there!*

# EPILOGUE

Unrequited love has always been a mystery to most of us. It is a paradox wrapped in longing, to carry the weight of pain, the ache of loss, and the silent suffering of what could have been. Yet, it leaves us with that one haunting question that passes like an inheritance through generations, lingering like an unspoken legacy woven into our very DNA.

*If it was never meant to be, why did it have to be?*

For years, I have wrestled with this question, turning it over like a puzzle with missing pieces. As someone who questions everything, who refuses to accept pain without seeking its purpose, I have walked through the fire of my own emotions, searching for answers. And through the search, I have found transformation. We are never truly the same before and after encountering such love. Sometimes, people are portals forcing us to confront the rawest parts of ourselves. And learning to hold something beautiful even when it is not ours to keep is the highest form of love I have ever witnessed in my life. Perhaps, the godly transformation that can ever happen to a human creature.

This book is a reflection of that journey of mine, because I wanted to be the kind of soul who gulped the unasked pain, swallowed the suffering and yet, instead of being consumed by it, wished to throw light for those who tasted the same. I hope it reaches you at the right moment and helps you find the answers you seek. Until we catch on with another transformative story,


Hugs.


Swati Mukilan.